PET PROJECT

MANOR DRIVE
BOOK THREE

KATE BAUER

CONTENT WARNING

This book contains graphic depictions/descriptions/recollections of Sexual Assault, homophobic slurs, suicidal ideations, family abandonment, racism, and mention of conversion camps and a failed restraining order.

Discretion is advised.

INTRODUCTION

Manor Drive is a secluded street, set atop a cliff and surrounded by forest, a mere twenty minutes outside of the city. The only way to reach it is the steep drive behind the roadside bar, McKinley's Tavern. The steep angle of the road, and its ascent into the woods, seem to be enough to deter the average person from trespassing. It is at the end of the road that you will find a large manor house, shared by likeminded young people... the house lovingly referred to as "Kink Manor."

The neighborhood on the hill used to be a trailer park back in the day, until the local landfill bought them out and forced the residents to leave. However, the company went bankrupt and the landfill covered before the grounds of the property were ever disturbed. For years, it sat empty and abandoned, nature trying to reclaim where homes once stood... until an anonymous buyer snatched it up at auction.

Within months, the road to the left of the hilltop was

revamped into a modern mobile home court, housing a dozen brand new homes. The road to the right, however, became the private drive for the manor house. The house is a newer addition, added around five years ago, shortly after the bar at the bottom of the hill changed ownership.

No one really knows who owns the small neighborhood on top of the hill, nor the bar next to the highway, but one thing is for certain – as long as it's legal, you're expected to let your freak flag fly.

1

DONNIE

THREE YEARS AGO

I never intended to set foot on a college campus again. Unfortunately, I needed to finish my business degree. When I left Tibalt University, I figured I would serve my probation and just move on with my life. The world had other plans.

At first, I tried to go back to Tibalt, but the dean there forced me out. When I applied to Pitt, I was waitlisted. Point Park would have required me to retake half of my classes. Wrenshaw was my last hope.

It turned out to be a good thing in a way that my dream school became a nightmare. I lost all of my scholarships with the guilty plea, but I gained the respect of a man who has since given me my purpose in life.

Mr. Jones took a chance on me, a kid with a record and a lot of bad press following him. He gave me a job. He taught me the ins and outs of running a coffee shop on a college campus, or rather just barely adjacent to the campus. He put his trust in me, and I could never repay that trust.

"Congratulations, Donald," Mr. Jones says, clapping me on the shoulder. "You did what you set out to do."

My own parents haven't even congratulated me on getting my degree, despite being the first in my family to ever do so. They are still ashamed of the fact that I snitched on my teammates. *I'm* ashamed that my family puts more importance on a fucking sport than on the integrity of their son.

Placing my degree certificate down on the desk in the office, I pull the old man into a hug. In the last year, this man has shown me more love and kindness than anyone else in my life, just by being present and holding me accountable to my shit.

"Now, now," Mr. Jones chuckles as he pulls back from my arms. "None of that sappy shit, Donnie, my boy. I still gotta give you your present."

He reaches into the safe to pull out an envelope and a set of keys. Mr. Jones always told me he was looking for someone to run the place on a more permanent basis so that he could retire, but I never thought he would promote me to manager after only a year.

"Mr. Jones, I really appreciate the promotion, but are you sure you want someone with my reputation as the manager?"

"For the last time, Donnie, call me Walt," the old man huffs as he pushes the items into my chest. "And who said anything about manager? I'm making you an owner."

Stumbling back into the desk, it takes my brain a little bit to reboot. Owner? There's no way.

Shaking my head, I try to hand them back to Mr. Jones... Walt, but he won't take them. He backs out of the office and heads to the front of the shop to unlock the doors.

"I'm not taking it back, kid," he calls out when I finally manage to drag myself out of the office. "If you don't sign, this place is closing next month. I want to be able to watch my grandkids grow up now, not be stuck here until they're old enough to go to college."

Pulling out the transfer paperwork, I realize, he's not just making me an owner, he's making me THE owner.

"I can't take this, Mr. Jones," I tell him as the first of what I'm sure will be many families start making their way into the coffee shop. "At least keep a controlling interest in the business. I can't be sole owner, not with my record. I don't want to tank your life's work."

The man chuckles as he hands off some fancy frozen coffee drink to a student before he turns to me.

"My life's work isn't this shop. That would be the two adorable munchkins about to enter kindergarten an hour and a half away from here. I know you'll do right by this place, kid."

I pull out a pen and sign the damn papers. Mr. Jones signs his part next. Then, the student with the over-sugared frozen concoction pulls out a stamp and signs for the notary. At my questioning look, the old man gives me a wink and takes the papers to the office to make a copy.

"And call me Walt, young man!"

2

SHILOH

THREE YEARS AGO

"Where did he come from?"

The drag queen keeps staring at me while I slink my way over to a shady booth in the corner to wait out the storm outside. I know I look bad, I mean beyond being soaked to the bone. Michael really did a number on me this time, but I deserved it, in a way. I spent so many years keeping my head down, fooling myself that I was safe as long as I wasn't noticed. I watched my step-brother destroy so many people in front of me.

Like father, like son, I guess.

McKinley's Tavern is a smaller, out of the way bar where they don't have a bouncer at the door. I figured no one would notice me when I ducked in to get out of the storm on my way home from the police station. The officer who took my statement offered me a ride, but there's zero chance I would be safe if Michael or one of his buddies saw me getting dropped off in a cop car.

I turned eighteen a few weeks ago. I figured after he nearly put his fist through my skull, I needed to get information to the cops about what he's got his hands in before he actually kills me.

Drugs, stolen electronics, counterfeit sneakers...

The jagoff even started to branch out into prostitution.

Last week, he brought home one of the girls from my high school. I'm pretty sure she was a junior in my study hall this past year. She just sat on the floor, leaning against the couch, eyes glazed over, drugged out of her mind. Michael got on a video conference and proceeded to take bids on her virginity, both from the people on the computer and the guys in the room with him. She didn't even flinch while he treated her like a product instead of a person.

I tried to ignore it. Better her than me, right?

Then one of the creepy old fuckers asked how much for *my* virginity. I thought my brother would tell him to fuck off. I thought he kicked me out of the room to beat the shit out of the asshole. Michael *never* let any of his friends put their hands on me. That's what I thought anyways.

I'm ashamed to admit it took me until two days ago when the creeper's hands were on my ass for me to realize the truth of why I was sent out of the room. I scratched the asshole's face up for his trouble. Apparently, that was the wrong response in my brother's eyes.

Michael was not happy about refunding him and

paying extra for his trouble. Then he made sure my face paid in kind when it met his fist, over and over.

I've been on the receiving end of my brother's fists since he got custody of me when Mama died around a decade ago. This time, however, he went harder than ever before. Since I turned eighteen, he decided not to keep the blows to places my clothing hides. Now that I'm no longer a minor, he doesn't have to worry about Child Protective Services showing up if someone from school notices the bruising.

Even then, my brother usually makes sure the bruising is minimal to where it is mostly hidden with my skin color. This time, even with my darker skin tone, there is no mistaking that someone had been whaling on me since my left eye is still swollen.

Mama being biracial meant she was *exotic* to the men who she loved. For me, it meant I got the mocha skin tone of my grandfather instead of the creamy ivory of my grandmother. My memories of them are little more than impressions at this point, but I remember the kindness in their voices… something I've been missing for a very long time now.

I don't know if I ever met my father's parents. He died when I was a toddler, and Mama was always too sad to talk about him. And my step-father wouldn't have let her anyways.

"You alright, kid?" the shorter guy behind the bar asks me as he comes around to meet me in the doorway. "You need me to call anyone to come get you? The cops to get the guy who mugged you?"

Shit!

I forgot where I was for a second. I'm being awkward as fuck.

Before I can open my mouth to answer, I see a huge man come out of the restroom to my left. He's easily a head taller than I am, if not more. Big man equals big pain in my experience. My body responds before I can even think about it.

When it comes to fight or flight, there is no fight in me anymore, not when it comes to people who look like *him*. I'm just lucky I didn't freeze, like I do with Michael... there's no point in fleeing from him. He always finds a way to bring me back – even the cops have had no choice but to put me back into his hands.

My brain shuts off as I tear off across the highway, lucky there is little traffic in this deluge. The next thing I know, I'm standing outside the shithole house where my brother and his boys run their business, pushing my hand through the coarse waves of my hair.

I shouldn't have come back. I should have found somewhere to hide out until the cops came to bust him. But my feet dragged me back here through sheer muscle memory.

Sometime in the last twenty years, all the big old houses in the area were bought up and converted into apartments. Michael somehow managed to snag one of these houses to set up his operation right before he got custody of me.

The front door is the one that hides the truth of what happens in this house. That's the entrance that faces the street and the only one that any legal deliveries are made to. The second floor, accessible from just inside the front door, he's been converting into a pseudo brothel since his favorite one got shut down and turned into some sort of dance club.

At least that's what I think he's doing there. I am constantly hearing sex and screaming from below my room. I've never been on that floor in the years we've lived here, and I don't think I want to find out after glimpsing some of the things his boys moved in there.

The top floor, formerly the attic, is *my* living space. Technically, I'm listed as being down on the first floor with Michael, but he can control me better being upstairs. The only way in and out for me is the fire escape down to the back yard, but with the motion sensor cameras my brother set up back there, I can't sneak out. Unless he sends me on an errand, I don't get to leave without repercussions. Now that I've graduated high school, I don't have enough of a reason to try most days.

I'm going to be in so much shit for today. It's my sixth... no eighth time sneaking out in the last year, outside of going to school. I should have gone straight back to the house after visiting the station. But the urge to visit and tour the new pet play room at the local BDSM club was just too strong to resist. I'm finally old enough to get in the door, so I had to at least try. The rain had other plans for me, though.

I will never forget when some girls in my freshman algebra class put kitten ears on my head and started petting me. To everyone else in the room, it was a cute joke. But to me, it was nirvana. In those few moments, I was able to relax in a way that I hadn't been able to since I was seven years old. I felt like I was back in my mama's arms. I felt safe.

I will do anything I need to in order to recapture that feeling, even facing the irate meth-head wanna be pimp stomping across the gravel toward me. Maybe I should have taken the cop up on the ride home after all?

"You've got a lot to answer for, boy," Michael snarls and grabs me by the back of my neck. At six foot nine and almost four hundred pounds, he is the spitting image of his father, the man who beat my mother to death in front of me. With every touch, every gravelly word uttered, I turn back into that scared little seven-year-old boy who was forced to watch the light leaving his mama's eyes.

Instead of taking me up to my small apartment, he drags me to the hatch for the basement. My feet are dragging through the gravel and grass as my step-brother pulls me toward the house. Yanking open the rusty slabs of metal concealing the cellar with one hand, he throws me down the stairs with the other. My head makes good friends with quite a few of the concrete blocks on the way down to greet the slimy floor.

Looks like he never bothered to call the plumber for the leak I told him about last month.

The slam of the metal cuts off most of the light in the room as I drag my sore body up off the grime. Shivering in my wet clothes, I make my way over to the dryer in the hopes that I forgot to empty it when I was doing laundry last time. Some dry clothing would be really welcome right about now.

Of course, the machine is empty. He's trained me too well, making me his house slave and all. Leaving anything in the dryer would be tantamount to stealing in his mind, not that he ever uses any appliances or knows anything about housework. I'll never understand how this racist asshole ever passed the background checks and home visits with CPS to be granted custody of me, but I gave up questioning it a long ass time ago.

Stripping down to my underwear, I throw my wet clothes into the dryer for thirty minutes on high. Crouching down next to the machine, I try and get at least a little bit of the warmth to seep through my skin. The rhythmic sound of my jeans tumbling around behind me somehow manages to lull me into sleep... or maybe it's a concussion?

The feeling of hands on my legs pulls me from my slumber and I shiver as my eyes focus, but not from the cold. Creepy Old Fuck is touching my nearly naked body while my stepbrother stands in the corner watching. My brain is slow to come back online. Somehow, I seem to have missed my underwear disappearing.

I push the wannabe rapist off of me and try to run up the stairs that lead directly into the house. That has to be how they got in here since I didn't hear the metal doors. But I don't make it to the door. Michael grabs me by the throat and slams me to the concrete floor.

"You *will* earn your keep, you little shitstain," he says while my vision is going in and out of focus like a kaleidoscope turning. "Now that you're eighteen, I don't get anything for keeping you around. Mr. Curry here likes a little *chocolate* with his perversions, so you get to entertain him."

I use what little movement I'm allowed to shake my head. I know he can see the fear in my eyes, and it excites him.

"It's him or the cross, boy."

I shudder at the thought of ending up on the wooden X-shaped contraption that I saw him moving up to the second floor apartment, but I'd rather be beaten bloody over Mr. Creepy with the rotten teeth touching me anymore.

"Cross," I gasp out as soon as the grip around my throat loosens. I know I'm not likely to get out of this alive, but I'll be damned if I'm going to catch herp-a-siphal-aids in this basement.

3

TOBY

THREE YEARS AGO

"I don't expect to hear from you until you have completed the program, Tobias."

I hold back my snort due to the fact that if my mother suspects even for a second that I am not going along with their plans to send me to this *"leadership retreat"* I will end up with a personal escort in the form of my Aunt Celia. She's the one who found the commune in Montana or Minnesota or one of those "M" states and convinced my parents that I need to learn how to be a proper man.

"I will do my best, Mother," I tell her with my fingers crossed behind my back before I climb into the car. "I will devote every ounce of my energy to completing my program."

I'm not completely lying. I somehow got a full scholarship to Wrenshaw University in Pennsylvania, that she just doesn't know about. I have every intention of completing my bachelor's degree program for business management with a dual enrollment at the local community college for culinary classes if I can somehow swing it financially. I'm going to open a café and bakery someday.

I just have to figure out how the hell I can get to Pittsburgh on my limited funds without anyone finding out and dragging me back to their "leadership retreat" in Wisconsin... is that where it is?

I tune out the rest of my mother's words as she lectures me on becoming a proper man and making her proud and blah, blah, blah. At this point, there's nothing more she can say that will twist the knife of betrayal any more than it's already been.

While my father is a stern man, I know *he* loves me, even with the fact that I came out as being pansexual. His only question was if I would still marry a woman and give him grandchildren someday. I was honest when I told him it will be a long time before he becomes a grandfather, and he told me it better wait at least until I can legally drink. I remember laughing at that, wondering how many times I drove him to a bottle or two over the years.

I thought I was lucky that my coming out was so uneventful, but of course my mother and her fucked up family had to ruin it. That very same night, she called either her sister or her father or some other uber bigot in her fucked up extended family and shared *my* truth with them. So, here I am a week later, getting shipped off to their little "retreat" community.

Father glances at me in the rearview mirror a few times during the forty-five minutes it takes us to get from our house to the airport. I didn't expect him to tell my mother to stay home, but I'm thankful he did. I don't want my last memory of the man I've always admired the most being tainted by her venom.

My heart drops when he pulls off into short term parking instead of just dropping me off. He helps me get my bags from the trunk and leads me through the parking lot.

"I'm going to get your boarding pass. Why don't you go grab us some coffees and we can have a little chat before you have to go through security."

I watch my father, the man I've looked up to for my entire life, go to the self-serve kiosk at the airline ticket counter and I struggle to hold back my heartbreak. I've watched the movies and read the books. I've read the blogs and know it's common, especially in extremely conservative families like ours.

Being disowned sucks ass.

I expected to lose Grandfather and my cousins. I expected to lose Aunt Celia, not that I think I ever had her to begin with. I wasn't even surprised at my mother. Disappointed? Sure, but not surprised.

I thought my father would still love me, though. I didn't think he would force me to go somewhere knowing they would abuse and torture me just because I was attracted to more than just women.

"Tobias? Did you forget the coffee?" Father asks as he holds out that damned slip of paper to me. Grimacing, I bring it up to my face. I guess I should probably know where I'm going so that I can figure out the cost to switch it over to...

"Pittsburgh?!"

My tears can't be contained as I throw myself into my father's arms. I'm certain the scene is making more than a few of the uptight pricks in the check in lobby of the Birmingham airport uncomfortable, but I don't give a shit. Not only is my father not sending me to a conversion camp, he is giving me his blessing to be myself.

"It's the last place your mother, grandfather, or aunt will look for you," he whispers as he crushes me to his chest. "Your Uncle Robert lives in around there somewhere. I'm not sure if you remember him from back before your Me-maw passed away, but he's a good man."

My father pushes me to the entrance for security and pulls me into one final hug. After releasing me, he hands over a folder. In it is information for a new bank account containing enough money to cover my living expenses for a while. If I'm frugal and keep my scholarship, I think I can make it last for at least the next couple years.

"I will always love you, Tobias. No matter who you choose to share your soul with."

My father's words give me hope that this goodbye isn't forever.

"I love you, Dad," I whisper the name I could never say out loud in our home before turning toward the TSA agent and my escape to my future.

4

DONNIE

ONE YEAR AGO

"Can I get some ice? And maybe borrow some chairs? And maybe a towel? Or a bandage?"

The rapid-fire questions coming from the boy in front of me make my brain hurt. Is this kid even old enough to be enrolled here? Before I can answer any of them, an older student I somewhat recognize comes through the door, carrying a smaller unconscious man in his arms.

My mind goes back to that night at the Streaker house, when I failed to help another person in help.

"Do you have somewhere I can lay him down for a few minutes?" the guy asks me. I recognize him as one of the pumpkin spice hating regulars now. "Lucky has this thing with blood where he passes out. Toby here practically ran him over outside, and as you can see, he got a bit scraped up. He'll be fine in a few minutes as long as I can get him cleaned up before he wakes up."

The first man, Toby I'm guessing, stomps his foot like a toddler throwing a tantrum before turning to me with a radiant smile.

"Whatdya say, hot stuff? Got a place to lie down in the back?" he says with an exaggerated wiggle of his eyebrows.

Rolling my eyes, I stifle the snort that wants to come out. The last thing I need is for a barely legal freshie hitting on me. I wave them behind the counter and down the hallway to my office. Shortly after Walt handed the place over to me, I put in the futon. More often than not, I end up needing to sleep in there while doing the books. Bookkeeping is not my forte.

"Thanks for this, Hastings," the taller guy says after settling Lucky on the couch. "He doesn't do well with being a spectacle."

Does this guy know me? I make sure I only go by my first name in the shop because of the notoriety of my full name in this area, especially among the universities. I guess my confusion shows on my face because the guy straightens up and pulls me aside.

"I was at the Streaker House party," he says as I feel like the ground has disappeared from under me. "I'm good friends with Eric. I know what you tried to do for him, man. If you ever need anything..."

I wave away his offers and head back toward the front of the shop, nearly knocking over Toby who is doing a shit job of eavesdropping. Turning away, I head for the back door instead. Maybe I should just throw myself in the dumpster and save everyone the trouble.

The past is catching up to me, and I'm not too sure I'm ready for it.

5

SHILOH

The bell jingling over the door makes me jump when I pull it open to enter the coffee shop on campus. Every little thing makes me jump since going to the pride event. Seeing Michael for the first time since he was arrested years ago freaked me the fuck out, but that was months ago. I stopped being the jumpy scaredy cat after finding my new family in Kink Manor.

Scaredy cat.

I chuckle at the unintentional pun that my brain conjured up as I join the queue to get some much needed caffeine. Usually, I can rely on Lucky to have a coffee ready for me since he drives us to campus on Tuesdays. But he sounded like he was about to lose a lung this morning with all the coughing. Spencer insisted he stay home and dropped me off here on the corner before racing back home to be with his boy. I hope it's not too serious.

I get it. I really do. They truly are a meant to be kind of couple, just like Eric and Matt. I don't think I'll ever have that for myself. It doesn't mean I can't be happy for them, even if I'm jealous as hell. The closest I've ever come to that is what I have with Toby, but we would never work like that. I've had to console myself into being just best friends with him, even though I want more.

"What can I get you?"

Looking up, I'm surprised to find I'm at the front of the line. I didn't even stop to think about what I want to drink today.

"Ummmm," I try and do a quick read of the menu board while the people behind me start grumbling. I didn't mean to make them wait longer. I only got lost in my head for a second.

"Just order already!" someone from behind me utters. "Some of us have places to be."

The stinging sensation in my eyes tells me that I'm about to have a panic attack, so I turn and run for the door. I hate the fact that I still have them whenever anyone raises their voice around me. My therapist says I've improved so much, but how much could I have improved if someone complaining about waiting for their coffee can set me off?

Hiding in the alley behind the coffee shop, I lose track of how long it takes for me to calm down enough to feel confident enough to face people again. Maybe it really is too soon for me to be out in public by myself?

SparklesTheUnicorn:
Mattie says he didn't see you in your class

U ok?

ShyKitten:
Can you come get me?

I was wrong

I can't do this by myself

PanPup:
Where R U?

I can skip my classes today and get us an Uber back home

ShyKitten:
Coffee Shop

But you shouldn't skip

Eli:
@PanPup if you skip another class, I'm taking away your Xbox

DaddySpence:
I'm sorry @ShyKitten

I wasn't thinking when I just dropped you off. Be there in ten minutes

SuperMattie:
@DaddySpence don't worry about it. I have a break in my schedule. Take care of your boy

> @ShyKitten I'm coming to you. Ask
> Donnie to make me my usual and pick
> something for yourself
>
> My treat
>
> **SparklesTheUnicorn:**
> Awww 😊 @SuperMattie to the rescue
> yet again
>
> **SuperMattie:**
> @SparklesTheUnicorn always your hero
>
> And quit changing the names in the
> group chat

Chuckling to myself, I throw a thumbs up emoji in the group chat and put my phone back in my backpack. One thing Eric is always good for is making me feel better. I don't know how he does it. Matt might be his hero, but he is the real hero. He saved me that night by not letting me run away after Eli pulled my ass off the street that night.

Wiping away the tears, I am thankful that I didn't inherit my mama's lighter complexion. At least my darker skin can more easily hide the fact that I had been crying. It's uncomfortable enough to get ridiculed for being a man that cries, but it's twice as bad being a black man who cries. I can't hide my ethnicity, so I try to hide my feelings instead. It doesn't always work when I'm also struggling with an anxiety disorder.

The dinging of the bell above the door when I walk back inside makes me jump again even though I knew it was going to happen. Glancing around the room, I notice it is relatively empty and heave a sigh of relief. It's bad enough that it was packed when I had my little freak out, but if there were any of those people still in the room, I would likely have to run off all over again.

"You alright, kiddo?" an older gentleman asks from one of the corner tables. "You look like you've lost a couple shades there. Pretty soon, you'll be as white as me."

I chuckle at the old man's borderline racist humor. I know he doesn't mean any harm. Mr. Jones was Mama's neighbor back before...well, everything. Looking at him now, the old man hasn't seemed to change at all, except maybe some more wrinkles.

"And you look like someone forgot to shake you when you came out of the wash, old man," I laugh and run over to give him a hug. "I've missed you, Mr. Jones."

I can feel the tears coming again, but this time I don't care. This man was the closest thing I've ever known to a grandparent, to safety, before I was ripped away – before the nightmares completely took over.

6

DONNIE

The commotion out front pulls me away from the conundrum that somehow was Walt's method of book-keeping. I have no clue how the man was able to keep this place in business for the last thirty years, but I need to make sense of these records it if I ever want to convince someone to invest in the expansion plans I have.

"Jessie? What's going on up there?" I call out to my opening barista and assistant manager. She is a great help and talented with the coffee, but her people skills could use some work. One of these days, I have to talk to her about it. I've gotten a few complaints, but I don't have anyone else capable to take over opening for me when I have things to do in the mornings.

"Some kid was holding up the line," she calls back. "I got it under control, boss."

Shaking my head, I get back to work. After another hour, I decide it's time to head out front to relieve Jess for her break since Tyson doesn't start until eleven. I'd rather not make Jess go for a full three hours before getting a break at all.

Walking around the corner, I notice Walt hugging a young man and whispering in his ear. The kid looks like he's crying, and something inside of me shifts.

I want to be the one to comfort him.

Hold on... What the fuck?

Nudging Jess with my hip, I ask her in a whisper, "When did Walt show up? And who's that with him?"

She shrugs before reaching under the counter for her vape pen. I have no clue what question she's shrugging in response to, but I don't push. She's not going to waste time now that I've given her the opportunity to get her nicotine in. At least the vape doesn't have the customers complaining about the smell when she comes back in.

"Hey Walt," I call out to the guys in the corner. "What can I get you and your friend there?"

The old man smiles at me but doesn't let go of the younger guy. After a whispered conversation, he gives me their orders.

"The professor's usual. My usual. And get this young'un a cookies and cream blender thing with extra whip and sprinkles."

The man in question pulls back from the hug with a look of shock on his face. I have trouble holding back my chuckle at the rosy tint darkening the deep mocha color of his cheekbones. I want to see that happen again. I want to *make* that happen again.

Ugh, I need to get laid apparently if I'm thinking of hitting on a very young friend of my former boss.

"You got it, Old Man," I call out as I carefully adjust myself with the heel of my hand behind the counter. I definitely do not need to be having thoughts like this for a guy. Instead of focusing on the question of whether his skin is as soft as it looks, I wash my hands and get started on the drinks.

The other couple of students who were loitering in the shop leave while I'm still fixing the frozen drink for Walt's friend. I'm about to take the drinks over to them when I hear the damn bell over the door. I hate the thing, but it's useful in letting me know that I need to put on my customer service act.

"Welcome to... Oh, hey Lew."

Professor Barnes waves absently while glancing around the room. When his eyes take in Walt with his young man, the tension in his body seems to bleed out of him. Turning back to me at the register, he gives me a smile.

"Call me Matt, Donnie." He pulls out his wallet to pay for the drinks at the end of the counter. "Those paid for yet?"

I wave away his attempt to pay for the drinks. "What good is owning a coffee shop if I can't give my friends a few freebies now and then?"

Chuckling, he gathers up the three drinks and heads over to the corner. I want to eavesdrop on the conversation, but that damn bell rings again.

7

TOBY

Shiloh needs me.

I didn't know Lucky was staying home today. If I knew that, I would have skipped my eight a.m. culinary class and gotten to Wrenshaw earlier. Tuesdays are usually fine. I leave the house at seven for my class at the community college, and Lucky takes Shiloh for their nine o'clock lit course. We all meet up at eleven for lunch with Matt and then I take care of my kitten until his last class of the day at three. Then the professor gives us a ride so that Lucky doesn't have to wait around for us.

My kitten needed me this morning, and I wasn't there.

Occasionally, the ride share drivers don't want to come out to the community college. It's tough relying on them, but I learned very quickly when I was sixteen that me and driving are not a good combination. I wrecked three cars before I was kicked out of driver's ed in high school. I call it my squirrel brain, but I think the official diagnosis would be ADHD if I ever bothered to get tested.

Focus, Toby!

As soon as the car pulls up outside of the coffee shop, I try to jump out. Slamming back into the seat, I can feel the heat creep up on my face while I reach down to unbuckle the seat belt. The driver somehow manages to limit his amusement to a slight crinkle around his eyes, so he's going to get a good tip for this. I might be embarrassed, but this is far from the worst thing I've done in the backseat of a car.

Racing into the coffee shop, I wince as the door makes a loud thud against the door stop thing and something from above goes flying halfway across the room. My brain takes a second to catch up to the fact that I just broke the damn bell off the door as I watch it roll toward the counter and the hot owner, jingling all the way.

He can jingle my balls any day of the week.

The flush that went away only a minute ago comes rushing back with a vengeance. Reaching down, I try to pick up the bell, but somehow manage to kick it instead. I spend gods only know how long kicking and chasing the damn thing around the shop, but the sound of a sharp whistle makes me stop.

Oh, shit! I dropped into pupspace in the middle of a damn coffee shop. In the middle of *his* coffee shop.

I might as well change my ethnicity to tomato at this point.

"Over here, Toby," Professor Barnes... Matt calls out. I am really struggling with the whole being friends with my professor thing. At least I'm not in any of his classes this semester. That would be really weird with him boning one of my best friends and all.

Standing up, I brush my hands off on my shorts and creep over to the corner where my friends are sitting with some old guy. If it wasn't for the fact that I already know most of Shiloh's back story and family history, I would think he was my kitten's gramps with the way they're sitting and smiling at each other. But Shy has no blood family anymore.

"Toby, I want you to meet Mr. Jones," Kitten says with an arm wrapped around the old guy's shoulders. "He lived next door to Mama and taught me all kinds of fun things when I was little."

"I taught you nothing, young man," he chuckles. "Plausible deniability is a thing, you know. Pleasure to meet you, Toby."

I take the old guy's outstretched hand and give it a shake. It's only polite, even if the green eyed monster is screaming inside of me because my Shiloh is smiling at him with no shadows in his eyes.

That's supposed to be my smile. And the fact that he's able to speak about his mama with this man without the fear...

"Nice to meet you, Sir," I say even though a part of me doesn't mean it. "How do you know Shiloh?"

Shy chuckles as he pulls me down into the chair on the other side of him. "I just told you, Toby. He lived next door. He... Mama let me stay with him when... Mr. Jones was my de-facto babysitter."

I'm torn at the sick sense of satisfaction that this old guy isn't the magic cure-all I thought he was. Why the fuck am I pleased that my kitten is uncomfortable?

It's because it means that this old guy isn't more important than me. Kitten still needs me the most.

"Squirrel brain," I mutter and take a lick of the whipped cream on top of Shiloh's drink. He never knows what to order and ends up with some overly complicated coffee that he doesn't even like. At least today, he got something in his wheelhouse. Cookies and cream is one of his favorite flavors. I'm constantly finding cookie crumbs in our bed.

"Toby is my best friend."

I look at the old man to determine how he feels about it, but don't think I did a good enough job hiding the flash of pain being called the 'best friend' instead of what I really want. Pitying eyes meet mine and for a second, I want to run. Away from here or to a safe place to start over, I'm not sure which. But one thing is for certain, my heart isn't leaving Shiloh.

8

DONNIE

Thank heavens the damn bell came down. I have hated that thing from the moment I first stepped foot in the shop five years ago. For the first few months, it was the signal that I was going to get sneered at or yelled at for my part in what happened to Lew...erhm, Matt's boyfriend back then. Over time, I managed to hide the cringe, but the feeling of shame and tension never went away. It's been forever linked to the damned jangling of that bell.

Watching the bell rolling all over the floor with the adorable man chasing it around on all fours was almost cathartic to witness. I've seen the guy in here before a few times. Each time he graces me with his presence, he definitely makes it memorable.

The first time he was in here, he tripped over someone's backpack and did some elaborate dance looking thing to avoid spilling his drink. In the process, he bumped into four tables and spilled about seven other people's drinks. But he saved his own and gave a little bow at the door before running away, red as a ripe strawberry.

The most memorable moment was probably the time last year when he knocked his smaller friend out cold in front of the shop.

"Donnie, get Mr. Squirrel Brain here a drink on me," Walt calls out, shaking me from the memory. "I'm thinking something decaf would be ideal."

"No fair, Gramps!" the excitable young man exclaims, running his hand through the sandy strands of his hair. "I need the caffeine to sit through my boring lit class later."

Lew, I mean Matt barks out a laugh before coughing in an attempt to cover it up. "I'll be sure to let Simon know you think his class is boring."

I spend the next few minutes observing the interactions between the men at the table while I come up with something that I think truly fits the smaller man's tastes. He acts like he is the personification of a golden retriever puppy, but I see the tension in his back every time Walt shows affection to the young man who had been crying earlier. There is something between the two of them, but he doesn't seem to know how to show it.

Carrying over the fruity monstrosity I just made up, I get raised eyebrows from both the professor and my former boss. So what if I want to make sure the guy gets more in his system than just caffeine? I can't help it.

"Too much caffeine means a crash later in the day," I tell him with a smile when he looks at me doing a decent trout impersonation. "Be a good boy and drink something healthy."

Matt and the guy they called Shiloh both break out in laughter while Toby returns to the color of a ripe tomato. A sound under the table makes me look, and I see his foot bouncing up and down on the crossbar of his chair.

Huh, he really is like a puppy, isn't he?

"Thanks, Donnie," Matt says when he can finally take a breath. "We'll get out of your hair so that I can get some food into these guys. Thanks for the drinks, man. I'll text you later about that thing."

The two younger men gather up their things and follow the professor like they are obedient pets and not people, and I can't help but smirk at the sight. Before I can question it any further, Walt clears his throat.

"So what is so important you needed to call me away from my grandkids?"

9

SHILOH

The coffee shop guy is probably the hottest guy I have ever seen, not that I actually look at anyone anymore. I remember when I first started to realize that I liked guys instead of girls. Frank was mad, but Mama assured him I would grow out of it, that kids didn't really think about kind of stuff until they were much older. I might have only been five, but I was certain that I felt things for boys that I was supposed to feel for girls and vice versa. But after Frank hit Mama for talking back, I kept that to myself.

Getting dragged all over campus by Toby is like second nature to me at this point. I love him dearly, but an introvert, he is not. After my morning freakout, I have resigned myself to having way too much attention thrust at me for the rest of my day, especially because my guard dog seems to think he is somehow at fault.

"So, I'm going to be here as soon as your class is over to get you and take you to Professor Barnes's office. He said we can hang out in there until he finishes up his last class around four, and then he'll take us back to the house."

Sighing, I look around the rest of campus as we walk toward the art building. I'm a junior, being escorted like a kid on his first day of kindergarten while freshmen two weeks into the semester are heading off to their classes with a kind of confidence I have never known. I would give anything to be able to feel comfortable walking across campus by myself. It's just too *public.*

At the entrance to the building, Toby gives me a massive bear hug before pushing me inside. He really must be feeling insecure if he's being this touchy feely in public. He usually avoids anything more than hand holding unless we're in a group or somewhere like the Devil or the Monarch Room.

"Remember to wait for me!" he calls out and almost trips over his own feet as he rushes across the quad to get to the building that holds his business courses. I look up at the ceiling of the entryway in exasperation. I love him, but he has got to stop treating me like a child.

I love him so much, but I can't be with him. I'll never be strong enough and then I'll lose him, just like I lost Mama.

Fuck! I feel the stinging sensation in my eyes again.

Ducking back out of the doors, I race off around the back of the building towards the small park adjacent to the campus. My art professors are understanding of my anxiety issues being exasperated with my stepbrother being out.

They won't make a big deal out of me being late or missing class as long as I check in and get the assignments done. I shoot off an email to my professor while wiping absently at my face. I hate being so out of control with my emotions.

Walking through the little copse of trees calms me in a way that little else does lately. In the woods, surrounded by nature, there is absolutely nothing that reminds me of my life before Kink Manor. That more than anything else brings me peace when my anxiety and PTSD flares up. My therapist says it's avoidance, but she can fuck off. I need these brief respites however I can get them.

My phone dings from my backpack and I pull it out to look at my professor's response. I'm surprised to see it's a text from Matt, outside of the group chat.

Matt Barnes:
Where R U?

Pup is about to get arrested

Me:
WTF?

Where is he?

What happened?

Matt Barnes:
Campus Security

Admin Bldg

Y aren't u in class?

> **Me:**
> Meet you there

I ignore the panic rolling through me at the thought of facing police in favor of getting to Toby as fast as possible. I can't lose him. Even though I know as a white boy with blond hair and blue eyes, he would be treated way better than I would by the cops, I can't risk it.

What if the rest of his family has found him?

Sprinting for the administration building, nothing is filtering into my brain other than the sheer need to get to Toby before he's taken from me. Maybe if I hadn't been in such a state of panic, I would have seen the wall of muscle in front of me before I crashed into him.

10

TOBY

After dropping Shiloh off at the building with all of the art studios inside, I race off toward my last class of the day. I'm late most days, but so is Professor Silas. She only takes attendance at the end of class and only because the school makes her. It's an easy A as long as I do the assignments.

Outside of the classroom, there is a bit of a commotion, but being on the shorter side at five seven, I can't see over the crowd. The sound of a slap makes most of the crowd part for someone to make a hasty retreat, and the drama lover in me creeps forward to get a good look.

"Bitch!"

I turn from the sight of the angry woman student stomping down the hall at the man's shout. I mean, yeah, she slapped him in public, but that's still no reason to be calling her names. Intent on giving the man a lesson in manners, I freeze at the sight of him.

He's fucking huge! I'm pretty sure he's taller than

Jace and solid muscle where our teddy bear has some cushion. This guy also has some tattoos that I'm pretty certain came from time behind bars. As he turns fully to face my direction, my fear turns to pure rage.

This is the fucker who hurt my Shiloh. This is Michael.

Before my brain can kick in and remind me that this guy can squash me like an insect, I race forward to sucker punch this ass-nugget in the balls. I must have caught him off guard because he goes down like a douglas fir in December.

"Timber, mother fucker," I grunt out and proceed to start kicking him anywhere I can reach. Too bad the asshole covered his head. I would love to stomp him until his brains leak out.

"Toby! Stop it!"

I can feel hands pulling at me, but I shake them off. I feel my elbow make contact with something with a satisfying crunching noise. This piece of shit needs to die for what he's done to my Shiloh. It's the only way to give him some real peace from the nightmares.

Arms wrap around me, trapping my hands to my sides and I'm lifted away from the whimpering shithead on the ground. I struggle against the hold that has me trapped and can't stop the animalistic growl that escapes my throat.

Someone leans in close to my face, holding a bloody rag up to his face. It takes me a few seconds to recognize Professor Barnes. Oh, shit. Eric's gonna kill me for hurting his Mattie, but fuck if I'm done with this asshole.

"Down, boy," he commands softly. "You need to calm down before you end up in jail. You haven't done any real damage to Greg, but you need to stop now."

The rage disappears in an instant. Greg? Who the fuck is Greg?

Looking past my professor turned neighbor, I get a better look at the guy on the ground. He's still big and tatted up, but now that I'm looking, he's missing the scar on his face and his eyes are all wrong.

"I fucked up," I mumble quietly enough that only Matt and the guy holding me can hear. "I thought it was *him*. I can't let him near my kitten."

Campus security shows up late to the party, as usual, and requests in a not very nice way for me to join them. They also help up the guy, Greg, to take him to the infirmary. There's a bunch of hushed conversations happening around me while I'm marched away from the classroom to face my doom.

I see Matt running to catch up to that Greg guy and his escorts while I'm doing the walk of shame alone. I assaulted a total stranger because he *slightly* resembles the man who haunts my best friend's every moment. I broke the nose of my neighbor slash professor slash kind of friend when he tried to stop me from making the first mistake.

Mother was right. I'll never be anything more than a screw up.

11

DONNIE

"They're a package deal, ya know," Matt tells me as we walk up the stairs toward his office. "Don't think I didn't notice you looking at them both."

I give him a small shove in response. I fight hard to hold onto the belief that I have no clue what the hell he's talking about. Both boys are gorgeous in their own ways. Toby is a little blond spitfire while Shiloh is everything soft. I'm not even sure of his ethnicity, but his glossy braids and charcoal eyes are perfection. If Idris Elba and Beyonce had a kid, he'd probably resemble Shiloh.

"I'm pretty sure neither of them are looking for an older ex con to be their lover."

Matt scoffs. "Ex-con? Really? You were given probation on a misdemeanor charge."

We both move to the side of the stairwell to make room for the girl racing down past us in tears. Before I can get out what I'm sure would be a scathing response to put him in his place, a commotion can be heard from the end of the hallway that girl just ran from.

As we exit the stairwell, we can see a crowd ahead and there is no mistaking the chanting of the idiots among them. Some dumbasses decided to get into it over a girl.

"This isn't high school," I grumble as we push forward through the students to get to the problem children.

When we clear the last of the onlookers, I freeze. Toby, the tiny wisp of a man that is always so happy and excited in my coffee shop, is beating the ever-loving shit out of a guy that is easily twice his size. This doesn't fit at all with the joyful man I've seen in my shop over the last couple years.

"Mother Fucker!"

Matt's muffled shout snaps me out of my inactivity. Toby must have hit him somehow because that is most definitely a broken nose. I've seen my fair share of them during my hockey playing days, so I grab the rag from my back pocket and throw it at my friend so he can try to not bleed everywhere.

As for the fight, it's pretty obvious that what Toby is seeing is *not* this hallway. I never would have imagined this man held this kind of anger inside of him.

Dissociative rage is something I've witnessed first-hand many times over the years. Hockey players aren't generally known for being calm and well-adjusted humans on the ice, or even off it in some cases. But we learn how to handle our anger in non-destructive ways if we want to be able to keep playing.

While Matt is trying to stop his face from bleeding everywhere, I wrap my arms around Toby and pray he doesn't break something on *my* body while I'm restraining him. I can't really afford to be serving customers with black eyes or missing teeth.

Something Matt says finally gets through to the smaller man and he sags in my arms. I hear him mumble something before campus security yanks him from my grip to take him away.

"Shit!" Matt mutters under his breath before pulling out his phone. His fingers fly across the screen before he pockets it and looks at me.

"Can you meet Shiloh outside the admin building and take him to the security office for Toby? The pup is going to need to see him before he will fully relax. I gotta go talk things over with Greg in the infirmary and get my nose checked out. I really want to avoid him pressing charges if I can manage it."

I nod and leave him with a pat on the shoulder. I can't suppress the smile when I hear his muttered, "Sparkles is gonna be so pissed."

While he runs off down the hall in the opposite direction, I head for the stairs. I need to head over to the administrative building and wait for the quiet one, Shiloh. It's the only thing on my mind, so I don't even see the blur coming towards me until he crashes into me. Reaching out, I barely manage to keep us both upright while we catch our breath.

"Just the man I was looking for," I say in response to his crazed look. "Let's go get your friend Toby out of trouble, shall we?"

12

SHILOH

How in the hell did I not see the coffee shop guy in my rush to get to Toby? And why does it seem like he's just as worried as I am?

"Matt is trying to talk the guy out of pressing charges, so we'll see how much trouble your *friend* is in and take things from there."

The hesitation before he said the word friend has me curious about how much this guy actually knows about us and Kink Manor. If I had to wager a guess, I would have clocked this guy as straight and vanilla as all hell. He doesn't seem to like pain, neither seeing it nor experiencing it based on what I've seen of him. He's too stand-off-ish to be a Daddy.

His holding the door is a pleasant surprise, even if it is only manners. Chivalry isn't something I'm accustomed to at all. I don't know if people just don't see me or if they think that as a black man I will take offense, I'm not sure. The Daddies in the house will hold a door for all of us, but this guy is focusing solely on me as we enter the building. It's a bit unnerving, yet also exhilarating to be the focus of someone as hot as him.

"Don't worry, Shiloh. They won't call the cops unless the other guy wants to press charges. I think we stopped it quickly enough to avoid that."

"How do you know my name?" I ask as we step onto the elevator to go down to the security office in the basement. Why this school decided that a literal dungeon would be a good place to put the security office is beyond me.

"Oh, shit," he startles at my question. "We were never really introduced, were we?"

I shake my head at him and feel the corners of my mouth tilt up in a smirk. Holding out my hand to him, I say, "*Officially*, I'm Shiloh Abrams. I live in a house with eight other guys, including my best friend, Toby. Wait no, it's seven guys now. Eric moved in with his Mattie."

The guy throws back his head in laughter as the elevator doors open and we step out into the dark hallway. The sound echoes off the walls and makes it a little less slasher movie vibes. I'm always jumpy coming down here by myself. After all, the black guy is almost always the first to die in a horror movie.

"My name is Don," he says as we wait at the desk for the security guards to come out of wherever they are hiding. They're never at the desk. "Don Hastings. I know Eric through some unfortunate circumstances, but Lew... I mean Matt and I became friends shortly after he started working here. He was one of my first regulars after I took over the shop from Walt. Too many people had me guilty by association or labeled me as not trustworthy because of what I did."

Aside from Spencer, there's only one other guy that Eric calls his friend outside of those of us who live on Manor Drive. This must be the guy who turned on his teammates for the sake of a stranger because it was the right thing to do. Hero worship or something like it must show on my face because he looks a bit uncomfortable and eager to avoid my gaze as the judgey guard comes out of a room behind the desk.

"Hastings," the guy nods with a sneer. "For the last time, we can't do anything about the vandalism since your shop isn't officially campus property. Unless you can prove the vandal is a student attending here, the administration won't do a damn thing but waste all of our time."

13

DONNIE

Ralph is just as pleasant as always, meaning not at all. I feel Shiloh tense beside me at the tone the guard takes with me, but it's nothing personal. He is just a grump for everyone. The event he is referencing is something that I brought up three years ago when I first took over for Walt, and it hasn't been an issue since. Ralph just likes to harp on the past because being security here at Wrenshaw is boring as fuck compared to some of the bigger schools in the city.

"Not why I'm here today, Ralph," I tell him blandly and grab Shiloh's hand to give it a squeeze. His tension is starting to make me nervous, and I've been around way worse guys than this big marshmallow. "Where's the kid you guys grabbed from Jupiter Hall? His roommate here needs to know what's going on for their ride home."

Shiloh's hand jerks in my grip, but he doesn't show any outward sign of his distress. In fact, he seems to have completely shut down in front of Ralph. When I glance up at the guard in question, I see a softness to his expression that I have never seen before.

"You shouldn't be living with someone with anger issues like that, Shy," he says gently while the guy next to me flinches. "The offer is still valid, you know."

I feel the tension in the muscles under my hand, but Shiloh shows only a soft smile on his face. There's a new chill to his voice when he says, "I'm happy with my living arrangements. Thanks though. Can we see Toby now?"

Ralph snorts and shuffles some papers around on the desk. Pointing us to the room they use as a drunk tank during games, he heads back to the room he had just come out of.

"Why the hell a kid that sweet wants to live with such degenerates is beyond me. He needs Christ in his life, not those damn heathens. God can straighten him out, I'm sure."

Ralph's mutterings barely register to me until Shiloh pulls himself away from me to curl up on a bench in the corner of the room we were directed to. Once my brain makes sense of what I just heard, I'm flabbergasted.

Did I seriously just hear the head of campus security say that he thinks he can pray the gay away?

Is Shiloh gay?

Wait.

That's not the important part right now.

"So how do you know Ralph?" I ask him to break the silence while we wait for Ralph to come back with Toby. "Spend a lot of time down here?"

He shrugs but doesn't look up at me. I watch as his

fingers start tapping out a rhythm against his shins. It seems almost involuntary, like a nervous twitch or stim response. Something about this situation is making him more anxious. Is it being stuck in a room with just me?

"I had to come down here at the beginning of the semester to file paperwork," he finally says, barely above a whisper. "They needed a copy of the restraining order I have against someone and said an electronic copy wasn't good enough. That guy was the one who took my paperwork."

Restraining order? I am going to need more information on that once we get his friend out, but I need more information.

"How does he know who you live with or that they aren't good Christians?"

Shiloh chuckles darkly before looking at me.

"You haven't heard about Kink Manor?"

14

TOBY

I have no idea how long I have been in this tiny room. If they thought it was going to calm me down, they were wrong on so many levels. I didn't know I was claustrophobic, but yep. I'm pretty sure I just discovered a new fear.

Let's just add it on to the fear of churches, my blood family, ants, and kangaroos. I don't even know what prompted that last one, but I remember running screaming from the room when Lucky pulled out an old comedy from before our time called *Kangaroo Jack*. At least the rest of them kind of make sense.

"You got someone needing a ride home," the fat preachy security guy says when he comes into the room to interrupt my complete and total freak out. "You need to let that sweet kid find a better place to live than with sinners like you."

Did he just? No...

The school wouldn't employ a religious zealot for a

position like this when they are pushing so hard to be seen as LGBTQIA inclusive. Even *I'm* not that dumb, and the dean is supposed to be a genius.

Grabbing me by the arm, the guy drags me over to the drunk tank and tosses me roughly through the doorway. I probably would have hit the floor if the guy in there hadn't caught me. My face has made friends with many a concrete floor over the years, but it rarely happens outside of pupspace anymore and never from being manhandled.

Turning my head to look at the doorway, I see the guard has a disappointed look on his face. The asshole seriously wanted me to get hurt!

"What the hell, Ralph?" the man attached to the bulging biceps holding me asks in outrage. "Is this how you treat students?"

Glancing at the face of my inadvertent rescuer, I recognize hot coffee shop guy. Why is he the one saving me? Based on the way the jagoff guard was talking, I was expecting to see Shiloh, not some guy I don't even know the name of.

A whimper from the corner pulls my attention and I push away from the hottie to rush to my kitten. Of course he's here. He would have come straight here when I didn't show up after class. He doesn't like it down here at all, but he would show up for me. It's all my fault and I feel like shit for subjecting him to this place.

"I'm so sorry, kitten," I mumble as I pet his head, letting his braids fall through my fingers. "I didn't mean to worry you. I wasn't thinking."

The two men arguing in the background are just noise to me. The man in my arms is all that matters. He flinches at something said by the other men, and it's like my switch is flipped again. Rage and a need to protect my Shiloh rises up within me.

"What the fuck is wrong with you?" I growl out, holding Shy as tightly as he will let me. "Can't you take that somewhere else?"

"*You* need to shut the fuck up, delinquent," the wannabe cop threatens me. "The police will be here shortly to take you in and then I'll never have to see your sinful ass again. This school needs to keep you sick fucks away from the normal people."

15

DONNIE

Did he really just say that?

"What the fuck, Ralph?! What do you mean by that?" I get in his way when he takes a step toward the two men on the floor. "I can admit that Toby here got a little carried away up in the hallway, but you're sounding like you have a problem with something more than him getting in a fight."

"Guys like him are what's wrong with this country!" the security officer shouts as he throws his arm out toward the corner. "They practice sexual deviancies and don't even try to hide them. Their whole house is full of nothing but queers and pedophiles and this sweet young man needs to be away from all of that if he ever wants to be accepted as a normal member of society and not a perverted thug."

Stepping back, I take a protective stance in front of the two men in the corner. I might not have been strong enough years ago to save one boy from my old teammates, but I sure as fuck am able to beat Ralph. I won't let this piece of shit anywhere near these two boys.

"You need to step away, Ralph," I warn him. "For the sake of the years you treated Walt with respect, I'm giving you the opportunity to back out of this peacefully."

The man steps into my personal space to glare at me. "You're just as bad. Turning on your teammates for the sake of some fairy boy. He should have found Jesus and changed his ways. Instead, he just drags others down with him. You both deserve every punishment the Lord brings upon your heads."

The outrage I feel toward the asshole in front of me is about to boil over when a throat clearing pulls all of our attention to the doorway. Matt is standing there, looking absolutely murderous, along with three other faculty members and that Greg guy from the hallway.

"What the fuck did you just say about my boyfriend, Ralph?" Matt snarls and takes a step forward. "Did you seriously just say that he *deserved* to be drugged and gang raped because he's gay?"

Ralph takes a step back from me to look at the people in the doorway. He doesn't even bother to hide his sneer as he looks at Matt before storming out of the room. If I hadn't been right in front of him, I probably wouldn't have been able to stop Toby from going after him. As luck would have it, I somehow manage to catch him up in my arms again when he turns back into a snarling ball of rage.

"I'll take Greg to sign the forms," Professor Michaels

says, pulling the large man with him back toward the desk in the hallway. Professor Silas shakes her head and pulls out her phone.

"Let's get these two somewhere that Toby won't get his ass expelled," Matt grumbles and pats me on the shoulder before reaching down to help Shiloh up from the floor.

16

SHILOH

"You doing alright, kitten?"

Matt's voice helps to pull me out of the numbness I started to sink into back in the dungeon of the security offices. I felt safe enough with Don, but the security guy always makes me feel a mix of fear and rage that I used to feel around Michael before he almost killed me. It's easiest to go numb around him rather than confront the reason behind the emotions in my experience.

Looking around, I notice we somehow ended up back in the coffee shop and I nod absently. I'm as alright as I think I'm going to get for today. Ever since I saw Michael a few months ago, I have been living on the knife's edge with my anxiety. I didn't realize it was affecting Toby this much as well.

"Where's Toby?" I ask when I notice he isn't next to us. Fear starts taking hold again at the thought of him being taken away from me. My leg starts to shake and breathing is getting harder. I can't lose Toby. I can't ruin his life too.

Matt puts his hand on my leg to stop the shaking and says, "He's in the dean's office giving a statement about the fight and what went down with Ralph, the security guard. He isn't in major trouble and will be back here soon."

"But what about the guy he hit?"

"Greg deserved a good hit to the nuts for what he did to his girlfriend," Matt chuckles and takes a sip of his coffee. "He never should have pretended to be someone else to sleep with her best friend at a party last year. She found out he's been seeing both girls since then, without them realizing."

The wink he gives me makes me smile. My love of melodrama is well known in the house. One of my most vivid memories with Mama consists of our daily dates to watch her soaps. I was too young to really understand what was going on, but I loved to watch her reactions to the insanity on the screen. After she died, it was one of the few ways I had to remember her without feeling pain or fear.

Sipping my hot cocoa, I let the warmth flow into me. It's still too warm outside for hot drinks, but the encounter with the security guard left me feeling cold inside.

"What's going to happen?" I ask in a whisper.

Matt sighs and leans back in his chair.

"Toby will get a warning for violence, but with what happened down in the basement, it will likely be verbal and not even recorded in his file. Greg will hopefully learn to be honest that he wants to be in a poly relationship with his future partners. And Ralph is going to be fired. The cameras in the rooms down there record sound as well as video, so the dean knows exactly what was said. It's a fucking massive understatement to say he is not happy."

I take another sip and ponder over that last part. If that's true, that means everything that has happened down in that place has been recorded. I wonder...

"How long do they keep the recordings before deleting them?" I try for a conversational tone, but judging by the suspicion on his face, I don't think I've succeeded. "Would they still have videos from the summer? Or last year?"

Matt purses his lips but seems to consider it before answering. "I know they regularly hold onto the last ninety days, but I'm pretty sure they have an offsite storage where they keep the older recordings." He narrows his eyes at me before asking, "Why?"

I explain to him the times that I've noticed certain students would get sent there for things like harassment and bullying of the outcasts in the student body, but nothing would ever seem to happen. I have spent a lot of time being invisible, and I notice a lot as a result. There have been a lot of violations to the school code of conduct that have been overlooked just because the perpetrator looks like Toby or Don, especially if the victim is someone who looks like me or is a woman or flamboyant like Eric.

"I'm pretty sure the officer guy threw out the copy of my restraining order as well," I tell him as the door to the shop closes.

"Well, *that* is getting rectified," a voice from across the room calls out, making me jump. I had forgotten we were in a public place. "The safety of all of our students takes precedence over anything else in my university."

Gasping, I duck down to hide behind the curtain of my braids. Why the fuck is the dean talking to me?

17

TOBY

Throwing my backpack onto the bed, I growl out my frustration at the situation I put us in. Not only did I overreact and attack some random guy, but I also added another enemy to watch out for when it comes to protecting my friends.

"Why am I such a fuckup?!" I yell into air.

"Maybe it's not you that keeps screwing up, pup."

Scott's voice from the doorway shocks a squeal out of me that has us both dissolving into giggles once the surprise wears off. Plopping my ass on the carpet next to my bed, I throw my head back on the mattress with a sigh.

"What's wrong with me, Scotty?" I ask him as he takes a seat in my gaming chair in the corner. "Why do I keep causing problems for everyone I care about? First my dad, now Shiloh. Next it will be you guys... I'm cursed"

Scooting the chair across the floor, Scott reaches

down to pat my knee before he leans back again. Adjusting his glasses, he turns toward the window with a pensive look.

"You aren't cursed, Toby," he says quietly. "You just have a habit of bringing things to light that should never have been hidden in the first place. You helped your father see how toxic his marriage was and you saved your siblings from the fear and shame your mother's side of the family would have put them through as they got older."

Shame and fear? Mother never made me afraid. Grandfather did a few times when I was too energetic, but not my mother. The only shame I've felt is that I couldn't be what was expected of me. But I never felt like I had to hide who I am. I was just disappointed that I couldn't be what they wanted for the eldest son.

"I can smell the burning from here," Scott chuckles. "You might not have felt that way, but do you honestly believe with you coming out that those assholes aren't going to double down on your little brother to be a proper man? You coming out to your father and shining the light on the bigots on your mother's side of the family lets Richie and Rachel have the freedom to find who they truly are as they get older."

"They're only seven," I grumble as I pick at the carpet. "They don't know what they like yet. I didn't think of anything like that until I was a teenager."

Eric pokes his head into the room and proudly exclaims, "I knew I was gay around the time I started second grade and was excited to get Valentine's Day cards from the boys more than the girls. My father didn't find out until I was eleven and got caught cuddling with another boy on the playground."

Shaking out my body, I know when to admit defeat on a topic.

"Alright, so my little brother and sister can grow up *knowing* their mother is a bigot. That doesn't mean I'm not a screw up."

Eric saunters into the room and plops down to sit on the bed next to my head. Carding his fingers through my hair, he gives a little scratch behind my ear that makes me twitch. The fact that I'm ticklish there makes pupspace even more interesting.

"You are the farthest thing from a screw up, Tobias, and anyone who says differently will have me to deal with," he says as he grabs my chin to force me to look at him. "You fucking shut down a conversion camp with Bob this summer. You saved fifty kids who were currently trapped in that hellhole and God knows how many others who might have been sent there for their 'leadership retreat' in the future. You didn't screw that up."

Pulling away from Eric's hand, I shrug. It's not like I really did anything. I could have reported them three years ago when Dad put me on the plane to Pittsburgh. Instead, I ignored it, too hurt by the fact that I had to cut off all contact with everyone I had ever known. If it wasn't for running into Uncle Robert at Pride in the City, I would have kept my mouth shut about it. Only Shiloh ever knew about the real reason I was hiding from my family before that.

"That was Uncle Robert, not me," I tell them as I climb to my feet to leave the room. "Just because I'm around when something happens, doesn't mean I'm responsible for it."

I shouldn't let them chase me out of my own room, but I don't want to hear how they all think I'm some amazing person. I'm nothing more than a fuckup who can't even protect the person I love more than anything else in this world. Today made it glaringly obvious I will never be the man that he needs. Maybe it's time for me to step back and let my best friend find someone who can actually take care of him the way he deserves.

18

DONNIE

Leaving Jess in charge of the shop for the rest of the day is an easy decision to make when Matt invites me back to his place to have a discussion about the pets, as he calls them. Shiloh looked like he was ready to pass out when Dean Winslow was talking to him earlier, so it was pretty unavoidable that I would end up making sure he was alright.

After Matt pulled in at his trailer, Shiloh jumped out of his backseat and ran to the big house across the street from the mobile home park. I had already pulled up on the street in front of the mobile home, so I was waiting for them. I had to resist the urge to yell at him not to run, as if it is somehow my place to police the behavior of a fully grown, adult man.

"He gonna be alright?" I ask Matt as he unlocks his front door and waves me inside with a nod. A squeak and the pounding of footsteps down the hall makes me realize that Eric must have been on the couch waiting for his boyfriend.

Matt only shakes his head with a chuckle as he hangs up his keys. The place looks a lot more lived in now that Eric has been officially moved in for over a month now. The old futon got moved into the office slash laundry room while the cheap particle board furniture got relocated to Jackson's place. Now, the living room boasts a matching couch and loveseat, glass tables, and three bookshelves filled with knick knacks and various fiction books, mostly LGBTQ romance books.

"You're supposed to give me a heads up when you're bringing home company!" Eric's voice calls from the back of the trailer. "I'm not wearing my makeup... let alone pants!"

Matt barks out a laugh as his boyfriend comes back into the living room, pulling on a silver crochet crop top to compliment his tie dye leggings. As the two of them share their intimate greetings, I go to the fridge an get a drink. I grab out a Sprite for myself and a bottle of water for Matt. I hold up a can to Eric and he shakes his head at me.

Alrighty then, it looks like I'm not going to be graced with his presence today. We're still working through how to really interact with each other. I saw him at the absolute worst moment of his life when he was his most vulnerable. I know things that he has never shared with anyone else, not Matt... not even himself. I can never forget the sight or those sounds, not in a million years.

"I'm only going because the pup is probably going to

do something stupid without intervention, and Scott is currently the most dominant one in the house," he says as he smacks Matt on the ass on his way to the back door. "Eli and Jace are doing inventory at McKinley's and Jay had to go to some mandatory meeting for the big box store of depression."

"Where is Spencer?" I ask as I lean against the breakfast bar. "He doesn't have a case, does he?"

Eric grabs his man-purse from the hook by the back door and turns back to face us with the door open next to him. "He took his boy to Urgent Care. He's worried it might be something serious since Lucky actually agreed to miss classes. *I* think he's overreacting, but if anyone deserves to be doted on, it's that little one...And I thought *my* parents were bad."

Matt legit growls at the closed door before plopping himself down on the couch and putting his feet up on the glass coffee table. Handing him the water, I take a seat on the loveseat and crack open my can of Sprite. I don't even know where to start, but apparently my friend does.

"So, are you interested in Shiloh, Toby, or both?"

I sputter and choke on the carbonated beverage before coughing up a lung in the middle of Matt's living room. Bubbles up the nose burn like a mother fucker!

"I'm not blind," he says with a smirk. "But like I said before, those two are a package deal. If you're only interested in one of them, you have to be cool with them sharing a lot more than society deems acceptable for grown men in a platonic relationship."

"Are they only platonic?" I ask when I manage to

catch my breath. "It feels like more when they look at each other."

Matt shrugs like it's no big deal and sips his water before leaning forward to snatch the remote off the table. "Even if they have feelings for each other, they'll never be able to make it work, not for long anyways. They need the same thing that neither one can provide."

After a few minutes of my silence, Matt finally glances away from the television to look at me. I'm wracking my brain to try and figure out what he's talking about. Neither of those boys look like they give a shit about money, race, or social status. They're obviously not homophobic considering who is included in their friends circle.

"You still haven't figured out Kink Manor yet, have you?" Matt asks as he mutes the show he had put on. After a glance at my face, he leans forward in all seriousness to tell me.

"This isn't my place to share, so I'm not going to give you specifics," he says. "But how much do you know about pet play or age play?"

I swear I can feel my eyebrows meet my hairline. Pet play?

19

SHILOH

Hiding out in my cave in the basement is usually calming, but today it just makes me feel like something is missing. Toby took off without a word. He just left after his meeting with the dean, taking an Uber back to the house. How do I make him realize I still need him without sounding like a pathetic freak?

Or maybe he doesn't want me around anymore...

That thought makes me curl into as tiny of a ball as I can manage with my five foot ten inches of gangly arms and legs. I have what they would call a runner's body which is surprisingly conducive to tucking myself away into smaller spaces.

Surrounded by my blankets and pillows, I cry myself to sleep with the realization that I'm going to lose him after all. Even if I could somehow manage to get over the shit that Michael put me through, today only proves that Toby needs more than I can give him. All I manage to bring him is pain and anxiety.

The feel of a warm hand massaging my hip slowly brings me back to the land of the living. I'm halfway into my kitten headspace, but I completely snap out of it when I recognize the touch as *not* the one person I want to pet me. My hand slaps out, seemingly of its own volition, to swipe the offending hand away.

"Welcome back, Kitten," Eric says with a smile in his voice. "Are you going to be human for me or is this a time for me to let you stay kitty cat for a while?"

Stretching out on my pillows, I let my brain switch back online even though I would disappear into being a cat forever if I could. I've fantasized so many times that shifters were real and I could have a fated mate out there to love and protect me. Hell, I was fantasizing about that way back before I ever discovered that gay werewolf romances were a thing.

"Hey Eric," I mumble as I lay my head in his lap. I'm not completely ready to be a person just yet. "It was a bad day. I thought... Toby almost got expelled because I've been so worked up. I've been thinking about moving into your old room to give him some space."

We sit in silence for a while, Eric gently running his fingers over my braids, occasionally scraping his nails along the exposed places on my scalp. It's soothing in a way that nothing else is and I find myself tilting my head to follow his hand when he pulls it away.

"I need you fully out of kitten space for this convo, kitty cat. Can you do that?"

Sitting up, I nod my head and wipe the back of my hand across my cheeks to get rid of any lingering tears that might be there. I don't want to have this talk, but if anyone in the house would understand, it would be Eric.

"I can't forget about the last time I saw Michael... before this summer, I mean."

Instead of asking me to explain, he just pulls me into a hug. "It will be alright, Shy. He won't ever get to you again. We won't let him."

Sniffling back the tears that spring up with his statement, I can't help but worry. That's the problem. Michael always gets me back, and he'll destroy anyone who gets in his way.

20

DONNIE

It's been a week since the fight, and I haven't seen Shiloh or Toby once since. Jess tells me they've been in when I'm not around, and Lucky seems to be the designated coffee fetcher when I am in my shop. Such is the case today.

"Buying for all three today?" I ask him when he reaches the front of the line. At least the boy has the decency to look embarrassed when he gives me a quick nod. "Let them know I'm not mad at them, alright? They don't have to worry about coming in when I'm here."

Lucky looks up at me in confusion. "Why would you be mad at them? Did they do something naughty?"

The wording of his question and the way he starts rubbing the corner of his shirt between his fingers makes me tense. When Matt gave me the breakdown on the various kinds of kinks that he's seen in and around the people who live in the house across the street, he mentioned something about age play and age regression.

I wasn't sure at the time who might fall into that category, but I'm pretty sure I'm seeing it now.

"Go sit at my special table, Lucky. I'll bring the drinks over once I clear this line," I tell him, handing him the pack of crayons I keep behind the counter for the few kids that come in around family visit days. His eyes go wide at the sight, but he follows my instructions, pulling out a coloring book from his backpack as soon as his bottom hits the chair.

It takes about ten minutes to clear the line before I can go over to the table I keep reserved for my friends, half hidden by the counter. I spend a couple moments just observing the young man as he sucks his thumb and colors what looks like cartoon animals in various professional attire. He seems to pay special attention to the cats and dogs on the page he's working on.

"That's cute," I say as I sit down across from him. "Are you coloring it for someone special?"

Popping his thumb out of his mouth, he doesn't look up to answer, but keeps coloring with intention. "Shy-Shy and Toby have been sad a lot. This is for them," he tells me before he looks up into my face.

"But don't tell Daddy. I don't want him to be sad that I gave someone else one of my pretty pictures."

Having said his piece, he returns his concentration to the page in front of him.

Shy-Shy? That must be Shiloh.

"Why are they sad?" I ask him as I sit across the table from him.

He shrugs and continues to color with his thumb in

his mouth. Glancing up at the clock above the door, I realize there's only ten minutes until the next block of classes, and I'm not sure if Lucky has one that he's supposed to be heading to.

"When is your next class, Lucky?"

He pops his thumb out of his mouth and pouts like I'm taking away his toys. I can't hold back the chuckle at how it looks for a grown man to be so purely innocent. This boy is so fucking adorable that I can understand why some guys would want to have a boy like this.

The sound of the door opening has me looking up into the panicked blue eyes of Toby scanning the room. He heaves a visible sigh of relief at seeing Lucky in the corner, but tenses as soon as his gaze lands on me.

You'd think I would be used to it by now, but the rejection from this boy hurts like nothing I've ever felt before.

21

TOBY

For weeks, I've been avoiding the hot coffee shop guy, sending Lucky in for the necessary caffeine. And I need the caffeine to be able to concentrate in class. I can't afford to repeat any classes if I want to graduate on time, and without taking out more loans. One of the conditions of my scholarship is maintaining at least a 3.0 average. I came dangerously close to fucking that up last semester with everything that was going on at the house with Eric.

It's not that I was distracted, but I wanted to help. I feel so useless all of the time. Even though I'm the one in culinary school, Scott does all the cooking and he's so much better at it than I am... not that anyone in the house knows I'm taking classes in the evening. They all think I have a part time job to help pay for school. I haven't told them yet that my dad has paid for everything for me.

Well, he at least gave me the money I needed to live

off for a few years. I was dumb for spending what I did on my pup gear, but I wanted it, and it was so hard to say no to Eric. He even offered to buy it for me, but I didn't know at the time that he was a bazillionaire. I couldn't let him hurt himself financially for something as pointless as pup gear, so I bought it, thinking I could return in as soon as it was received... only to find out that pup gear is categorized as fetish items which are non-refundable — only able to be returned for a replacement due to defects.

I don't regret being able to fully sink into pupspace at the DC, but the cost of the gear forced me to look into student loans, which I can't even get. Mother has too much money, and Dad makes slightly too much for me to be able to qualify for any type of aid. This whole needing to be twenty three to be considered financially independent bullshit is really just another way that the government wants to keep the wealthy people ahead.

You are part of the wealthy, you dumbass pup!

Shaking my head to clear out the self recrimination, I have to actively stop myself from arguing with *myself* in my own brain. Comfortable isn't wealthy. I mean, yeah, I never had to worry about food, and every year we went on vacation, but it's not like we had a mansion or anything. I went to public school like everyone else...

Shiloh wasn't comfortable.

Pushing off the wall I was leaning against, I trudge off to the coffee shop. Matt dropped me and Lucky off here, but took Shiloh over to the security office to take care of his restraining order situation. I didn't really notice earlier, but Lucky was a bit too close to little space this morning since Spencer seems to have caught whatever bug he had a few weeks ago.

Glancing at my watch, I can see that I only have about fifteen minutes to get across campus to get to my administrative basics course. I might not need this particular course to graduate – it is one of five options for an admin course in my major – but I can't financially afford another semester or even another course.

Racing inside the coffee shop, I don't see Lucky. Did he need the bathroom? I let my eyes do a sweep of the room and they land on the back of my roommate as he's hunched over a table, focused on something in front of him... Is he coloring?!

Fuck!

Daddy Spence is gonna kill me for leaving him alone to the point he entered little space in public without anyone around to guard him.

Movement at the table makes me finally notice the one person on this campus I do NOT want to be seeing at this point in time. Well, maybe not the *only* person, but close enough. Hot coffee shop owner dude is so not on my bingo card for today.

"Toby, right?" he says as he stands up from where he was talking with Lucky. "Why don't you join us? Unless you have to rush to class..."

Oh, sweet baby Jesus, I could listen to him talk all day every day.

Wait! Class!

Fuck!

"I need to get to class," I mumble as I grab the to go cup with my name off the table and race for the door. "I'll pick up Lucky after to get him to his classes. Don't tell Daddy Spence, okay?"

Shit! I didn't mean to say that last part as I trip over nothing going out the door. Doing some weird hop skip thing that my body does, I manage to not faceplant on the concrete and race off to my boring ass admin class.

Way to make a fool of yourself in front of the hot coffee shop owner dude, Tobias. Oh well, at least I can help push him toward Shiloh. He needs a handler who can do the soft touches, and based on how he was reacting to Lucky, this guy might be the real deal.

I just hope I can make it to graduation before I lose my best friend to love. Maybe Scottie will be willing to play with a pup sometimes once Shy has his person?

22

SHILOH

"Because of the nature of the restraining order, we can only protect and enforce it if he should come on campus," the scary security lady says with a frown. Even though she is inches shorter than me and looks like someone's kid sister at first glance, this lady would send even Eli to the corner and not flinch.

"What are the parameters we need to watch out for, Cheryl?" Mattie asks her while I am doing my best not to hide behind him. I'm glad Eric lets me borrow him on campus. Ever since Daddy Spence graduated last year, it's been tough feeling safe away from the house, especially with knowing that my brother is out there somewhere.

"... the coffee shop is the only location off campus that would be considered a part of the protection because of the deal struck with the previous owner."

I zoned out of most of their conversation, but my

mouth started with the words before my brain caught on.

"Mr. Jones made a deal? Why did the mean fat one say he couldn't do anything?"

The lady, Cheryl, startled a bit like she forgot there was another person in the room before giving me a soft smile. Huh... she's not so scary when she smiles.

"Walt arranged with the dean to make the coffee shop a safe haven. That deal was never rescinded and the former employees of this office let their personal issues override their responsibilities when Mr. Hastings came to them for assistance with some vandalism. Basically, the shop is a place provided where any student, faculty member, or visitor can go to seek safety and asylum in the event of being targeted."

My brain takes a bit to catch up to what she is saying. Mr. Jones set up a sanctuary space just off of campus...

"Why?" I whisper to myself, not expecting an answer.

"Guilt," Cheryl replies with a sad look in her eyes. "He spoke to me often of a boy and his mother that he failed to protect a long time ago and wanted to make sure people always had a safe place to run to."

Matt and Cheryl continue going over the details of the security plan they are putting in place for me, but my brain keeps coming back to what she just said.

Mr. Jones blames himself for what happened to Mama? It's not his fault. It was mine.

He couldn't have known what was going to happen when he left to visit his kids. I mean, he was becoming a grandfather for the first time. Of course, his place was with his family that night. The only thing he could have done was die beside her that night, and I'm glad he didn't. His grandkids need him. He's a good grandpa.

"Shy? Kitten?"

Matt's hand on my shoulder startles me into folding in on myself. He rapidly pulls his hand back and steps away, waving at Cheryl to step back as well. It looks like Eric has given him instructions on how to deal with my trauma responses.

"Not a flashback," I mumble as I pick my backpack up from where it dropped. "You just startled me a bit."

"Alright, Kitten," Matt says and leads me out of the office. "Let's pick up Lucky and we can hang out with Don for a while until your class at eleven. The pup should be in class by now, and without him around, you guys can be spoiled with some sugary goodness."

Don...

Oh, man...

I let Matt steer me across the quad towards the one building I've been avoiding at all costs over the last few weeks. Don Hastings is the man that Mr. Jones handed the shop to when he decided to move closer to his grandkids. He is also the man who makes my inner kitten purr at the thought of his hands on me.

But I don't need a handler. Cats are solitary creatures. Plus, I saw the way Toby looked at him. I can't compete with that. It's better to admit defeat now.

"I think I need to move out."

Matt stops mid-stride, but I pretend not to notice. I

didn't mean to say it out loud, but now that it's out there, I can't help but feel it's the right decision for me. Toby needs to be free of my problems, my nightmares. My family at Kink Manor needs to be safe from Michael.

And maybe, just maybe, I can trick Toby into spending time around Don and make them realize they are perfect for each other...

23

DONNIE

"Absolutely not!"

Eric's voice is shrill as he storms into my office at the coffee shop.

When Matt came in with Shiloh earlier and realized that Lucky was in full little mode, he called for his boyfriend to come pick him up. From what I understand, the boy is only auditing elective courses this semester to figure out what he really wants to have a degree in. He almost has the credits to graduate, but he isn't sure if he wants to just yet.

"I won't allow it!" the crazy man in the sequined tank top exclaims as he flops himself onto the futon. "My kitten is not allowed to leave home,. He is safe with us."

I flinch as the memories of how I failed to keep Eric safe roll through my head, and he notices. Oh, God, I hate that I was so fucking weak back then.

"I'm sorry," I try to keep my voice even. "I tried so fucking hard to stop them, Eric. I can't ever make it right. I know that. I'll pay for it for the rest of my fucking life."

Eric's arms wrap around me from behind, cutting off my millionth apology, and it's just too much. I let my head fall to my desk and sob. The pain and the fear I felt that night are nothing compared to the guilt and failure I feel every single day. Even if they hadn't broken my leg and collarbone, ending my hockey career, the community's response ended my faith in humanity.

"You suffered, too," Eric whispers in my ear before walking back to the futon. "They destroyed both of us that night, but I've decided to stop letting them control me. You need to do the same, Donnie."

Lifting my head from the desk, I try to look him in the eye but fail. Leaning back in my chair, I stare at the ceiling and contemplate my answer.

"I couldn't stop them. I have to live with that every day... the sounds, the images, the smells... The things they were saying... The look in your eyes, pleading with them to stop.

"Eric, I see it every fucking night when I sleep and every time someone comes in my shop talking about the team here, I have to leave the counter to my employees. They got a fucking slap on the wrist for being fucking lemmings and I'm the one that the community punishes to this day!"

I glance over at the man on my futon to see tears glistening in his eyes.

"Don't you fucking cry over me!" I say, jumping up to pace. "I deserve it all for failing to save you. I knew they were planning on drugging you. I knew you'd be helpless..."

"I remember," Eric mutters, stopping me in my tracks. "I remember you saying you guys were only supposed to drug me and leave me in the room. I remember cursing you all out in my head for being dumbasses to not realize that if you wanted money, I could pay you literally a million times what that bitch Sabrina Carlisle could ever dream up."

He gets up and grabs me by my shoulders to face him. I've got a few inches on his roughly six foot height but the look he levels me with makes me feel like I'm about two inches tall.

"I also remember the sounds of your bones breaking as you tried to fight them off of me... the sounds of your choked gasps for breath when they were strangling you to keep you from calling out. Those were your team-mates, your brothers on the ice.

"I know the pain of betrayal when your family turns out to be the last people you can trust. My own father tried to kill me. But you lived. You got help for me. Spencer found me because of you."

Shaking my head, I step back. "I didn't get help. I woke up in the hospital."

Eric uses his thumbs to wipe the moisture from under my eyes as he steps back into my space. "You fell down the stairs, crawling through the house to find someone to help. Spencer saw you and called 911. He said before you lost consciousness, you told him about me in the room. He left you with his future frat brother and ran to find me. Without you, no one would have found out about any of it, and I wouldn't be here at all today."

Staring into the face of the main I failed so epically, I can't accept his words. I don't remember seeing Spencer at the party at all, let alone telling him about what happened in that room. The only reason I'm not completely writing it off is because Spencer himself told me he remembered seeing me at the party.

Pushing it down to deal with another day, I pull back from Eric and resume my seat at my desk. "So what are you objecting to today?"

Changing the subject will work so much better than facing those feelings.

It takes Eric a moment or two to realize I've shut the door on discussions regarding my guilt, and I can see the instant he remembers why he flew in here in such a tizzy in the first place.

"Shiloh is not moving in here," he proclaims like the royalty he believes himself to be. "my kitten is not equipped for living alone."

24

DONNIE

Kitten? I totally thought when Matt explained the pet play thing to me a few weeks ago that it was referring to Toby as a pup. I did a bit of online research and saw that pups and ponies seem to be the most popular in the pet play subset of BDSM. And if there is any person I've ever met that embodies a puppy, it's Toby.

"Did your boyfriend have a chance to explain before you jumped in your mini cooper to demand I rescind my offer of a place for Shiloh? Did you ask the man himself why he wants to move?"

Eric sniffs haughtily and lifts his chin while giving me the side eye. Yep. He didn't even wait for explanations before coming over to read me the riot act.

"For your information," I say with exaggerated slowness. "Lucky dropped into little space when he came in for their coffees. Before you ask, I don't know if anything triggered it. Matt already gave me the third degree about it earlier. Toby rushed in, grabbed his coffee and almost killed himself tripping over nothing on his way out the door to get to class, so I couldn't ask him about what to do. Lucky was content to keep coloring, so I sat with him until Matt and Shiloh came in."

Thinking back on it, I relay the events of when the two men came in to the shop, obviously not on the same page about something.

"You can't move out of the house!" Matt says in a hushed tone, visibly holding back from touching the smaller man.

"I might not be strong enough to protect my family by myself, but I need to be somewhere that the restraining order will keep him away completely."

Restraining order? I get up from the table, surprising Lucky with the movement as he turns to the two men who just entered.

"You can't live alone, Shiloh," Matt says, not noticing the little who is actively paying attention to their argument. "The guys would never agree. Plus, where would you find the money to break your lease?"

"You're leaving us?" Lucky cries out and rushes toward his friend. "You can't leave me, Shy-Shy! You can even have my Daddy if you want, but please don't leave me!"

Shiloh just holds onto Lucky while he sobs. I'm glad that the shop is relatively empty this morning, and the people who are here seem to be familiar with or don't have the energy to care about this drama happening in front of them.

"Drama at Kink Manor. What else is new," Jess

mumbles sarcastically from behind the counter, and I have to fight back a sneer towards my head barista.

"I have to leave," Shiloh says, pulling my attention back to the scene that has turned my shop into a telenovela. "The house is too far away for the cops to get there if Michael decides to show up. There's too much opportunity for him to hurt someone with me being out there. I just need to find a place close enough to campus to where I only have a short walk to be protected."

A short walk to campus? Protected?

"Excuse me," I interrupt before Lucky can start wailing again. "Can someone please fill me in on what is going on in the middle of my shop?"

With a sigh, Matt explains the situation of Shiloh having a restraining order out against his stepbrother who was recently released from prison. The two of them had just come from a meeting with the head of campus security over what the school will be doing to protect him.

."... and then this headstrong kitty decided that he needs to live away from everyone who cares about him, like we can't keep him safe"

Before I can say anything, Lucky pulls back from his friend and stomps his feet in protest.

"My Daddy is the bestest at keeping people safe! Or... well..." I watch in wonder as I can see the man overtake the little. I can't stop my mind from trying to decipher what it is that pulled him out of his little space. "Actually, counting on Spencer and Eli might lead THEM to get into trouble."

Shiloh holds his hand out towards the smaller man and gives Matt a look as if to say, "See?"

Matt sighs and looks to me for help, but Lucky bulldozes over me again.

"But you can't get a lease or anything in your name or else el douchero step brother-o will be able to track you down. I'd say you could stay at Gramps's place but that's really far away from school and you'd be vulnerable with having to Uber it back and forth to school."

Before anyone else can interrupt, I blurt out my solution with a little less tact than intended.

"There's an empty room in my apartment upstairs!"

25

SHILOH

After clearing it with my professors, Matt drops me at home so that I can start packing up my things... the house. This isn't going to be my home for the foreseeable future. Michael saw to that.

"What's up, kitty cat?" Scott calls to me from the doorway. "What's with the boxes?"

I don't know what to tell him, so I just continue to pack, ignoring the burning sensation in my eyes. I explained to Matt that I wanted to get moved before telling anyone in the house because I know I'm not strong enough to stand up to them if they all try to make me stay. They need to understand like Lucky did. I thought it would be harder to convince him, but he gets it.

"Shy? Talk to me kiddo," Scott says as he squats in front of me. He doesn't look it, but he's the oldest one out of all of us in the house. He's shared a little bit with me about how he ended up here because I needed the help to realize that I didn't *have* to do all of the domestic chores in the house to earn my keep.

Putting the last of my kitty toys into the box, I look up at the man who is essentially my true big brother and I can't stop the tears from falling.

"I'm moving out," I tell him as I get up to place the box of cat toys with the rest of my stuff. Pulling open the closet door, I let out an audible sob at the sight of my kitty collar hanging next to Toby's pup collar.

I feel arms come around me and for once I don't tense up. Usually, it's only Toby that can touch me without fear of pain overwhelming me, but I guess my body finally recognizes Scott as someone who won't hurt me.

"You're only going across the hall, right? Toby will understand."

I turn around in his arms and clutch my brother to me. Even though I'm taller than him by a couple inches, I want to disappear into his arms. I make myself smaller and let all of my pain and fear out while he rubs soothing circles on my back.

When I finally slow to just hiccups, Scott pulls back and wipes the moisture from my face using his sleeve.

"Feel better, kitten?"

I nod and sniffle, rubbing my nose with the back of my hand, wanting desperately to drop into kitten space. But I have to stay human. I have to explain... especially if I'm going to enlist his help to get out of here before everyone is back.

"I'm moving out of the house — away from Manor

Drive," I tell him and flinch at the pain I see on his face before he puts up a mask of professionalism. I forgot...

"I'm not leaving you guys!" I rush to tell him. "I just found somewhere I can be better protected until the whole Michael thing is taken care of in a more permanent way. I'm doing it to keep everyone safe."

Scott just nods woodenly and turns toward my pile of boxes. Grabbing a few in a stack, he heads out the door and turns toward the stairs.

"I'll drive you," he says before stepping away with my things and I hear the rhythmic thump of his heavy steps going down to the first floor. Scott never thumps...

"Scottie says you need help getting stuff to his car?" Jace asks as he peeks his head around the doorway. "Donating stuff?"

"Something like that," I mumble as I watch the big teddy bear gather up the rest of the boxes in one go and head for the stairs.

Pulling my collar down from its hook in our closet, I sniff and swipe at my eyes one last time. I'm doing this for Toby. He'll understand in the long run.

26

> **PanPuppy:**
> I don't need a ride today. Got called into work.

I throw the message into the Kink Manor group chat and hope no one questions it. As a condition of my not getting expelled for violence last month, I have to start meeting with a counselor for anger management. I told everyone in the house that I got off with a warning. I mean, I did mostly. Counseling isn't exactly a punishment.

Going to one on one counseling is definitely cutting into my discretionary funds, but it's the safer alternative. I could technically attend group meetings for free at the community center, but there's a good chance that meetings are a condition of Michael's parole. At least, that's the case in all of the television shows.

"Tobias Walker?"

I jump up from my seat in the hole in the claustrophobic waiting area and head for the disembodied voice coming from the now open door.

"Is the room out there so tiny to keep you in business?" I ask no one in particular as I glance at the childish artwork on the walls in the short hallway. I didn't bother to make note of what all counselling this Doctor Monroe did. They were just the cheapest option that covered anger management and was also covered by my insurance.

The woman's laughter from the room to my right pulls my attention away from the unique drawing of what looks like a dog eating a person with another person on their back.

Stupid ADHD...

The lady finishes rounding her desk and takes a seat before motioning me to sit across from her. "You're not the first to think it, but you are the first to outright ask at the first session."

"You're Doctor Monroe?" I squeak and sit like I was dropped from a plane to land in the rather uncomfortable pleather monstrosity one might call a chair. The woman in front of me looks to be barely twenty and gorgeous to boot. My inner puppy is panting at how hot she is.

Down, Boy!

She chuckles as she opens a folder and picks up her pen.

"Thank you for the compliment, Tobias," she says and I wince to realize that my inside thoughts did not stay inside my head. "But I am a very happily married woman and before you ask, I am certain my wife is not the sharing sort."

I gulp and start shaking my head maniacally. "I didn't... I wasn't... I mean... You're... and I'm... and Shy..."

Shiloh...

I grab the armrests of the chair and take a deep breath before starting again.

"You are drop dead gorgeous and I will never deny that, but there's already someone in my heart that means more to me than anything else in the world and until I get him settled with someone who deserves him, I won't ever look for myself."

Doctor Monroe looks up at me with an eyebrow raised.

"Why don't you think you deserve him?"

Of course, she had to pick up on that. Let the fun begin...

An hour later and thirty bucks poorer, I'm emotionally wrung out. Powering on my phone, I pull up the rideshare apps to determine if Uber or Lyft is getting my money today. With how far out of the way this office is, I'm looking at a fare of at least thirty bucks to get back home. Seeing that Lyft has the shorter wait time, I cancel my Uber request before I lose even more money and crouch down against the wall of the building to wait.

Zoning out, I let the twenty minute wait pass while ignoring the world around me. I even ignore the pings of the house group chat while they are all discussing something. It's about dinner time, so it's probably just Scott calling everyone to eat. It's not like me going to "work" is big news or anything. Maybe Eric is up to something?

The honk of a horn shakes me out of my musings and I look down at my phone to see my Lyft has arrived. I always double check the name of the driver, ever since I got into the wrong car after class one night and ended up having to pay for two trips when the other person just stole my ride and the driver didn't bother to fix it.

My driver is… Jay?

Glancing up at the car idling against the curb, I see the disappointment on my roommate's face as he stands in the open door of his newish car. He had to trade in the vamp cruiser last month after it finally kicked the bucket. I forgot he's driving such a nondescript vehicle now.

There's no hiding it now…

I shuffle toward the car and drop into the backseat in embarrassment.

"As much as I'd like to lay into you, Pup," Jay says when he pulls away from the curb, "I'm not going to. I reckon you're having a shitty enough day as it is if Shiloh moving out has you going to therapy already."

"HE WHAT?"

27

DONNIE

As soon as the drama queen exited my office earlier, I went online to order a bed frame, mattress, and other bedroom furniture that I needed to be able to turn the second bedroom into a proper second bedroom. I really shouldn't have offered it until I had already set it up, but I wanted to stop the free show happening in my place of business before I had to fire one of my best employees for saying things she really shouldn't be saying.

Once everything was ordered, I headed up to the apartment to get to work on cleaning out the room. The furniture wouldn't get here until tomorrow at the earliest, but I can at least get rid of the crap in the room before it does. As I open yet another box of hockey memorabilia, there is an alert for the video doorbell I installed in the alley. I only use that door when the shop is closed. But after the last year with the vandalism, any time someone is in the alley, I will get an alert.

When I open the app on my phone, I see my new

roommate, surrounded by boxes, waiting patiently at the door.

What the fuck?

Racing down the back steps, I fling open the door to see Shiloh standing there with a sheepish smile on his face, worry plain in his eyes.

I look to the sky for guidance or patience or something and take a deep breath before waving him in. He does this little wiggle shimmy thing that makes me smile before he grabs a pile of boxes and bounces up the stairs. I grab a two by four from under the stairs to prop the door open and move all of the boxes into the small hallway before putting the piece of wood back under the stairs and making sure the door is locked.

Shiloh comes back down the stairs and looks shocked to see everything inside and the door closed.

"I'm sorry. I should have called first... or made sure you were home... or made sure you really wanted me here..."

Eric warned me that the Shiloh doesn't like to be touched, so I just pick up a stack of boxes and nod for him to grab some more himself. The small lifting of the corners of his mouth gives me some warm fuzzy feelings that I'm not quite ready to explore just yet.

It takes us less than ten minutes to get all of Shiloh's things into the apartment. For now, I put his boxes in a corner of the living room. I don't want to risk them getting mixed up with the trash I'm pulling out of the room that I'm setting up for him.

"The furniture and stuff won't be here until tomorrow," I tell him as I set down the last of his boxes. "I just have to take some boxes out to the dumpster and move some stuff into storage downstairs. Then we can move your boxes into the room. You can take my bed for the night and I'll stay in the office on the futon."

Shiloh starts shaking his head frantically before I even finish talking, but I give him what my mom always referred to as "the look" and he stops.

"Look, it's not the first time I've slept in my office. It's fine and regardless of whether you sleep in it or not, the bed is yours for tonight."

The gorgeous younger man stares at the floor but nods. It's difficult to tell with his darker complexion, but I think he might be blushing again... interesting.

28

SHILOH

I can't take the man's bed!

Then again, he did kind of demand it.

FUCK! I can't do it! He's for Toby!

While Don is downstairs taking care of the closing duties for the coffee shop, I pull out my phone and notice a shit ton of notification for the Kink Manor group chat that I've missed.

Eric:
FYI yinz better not give @shiloh any problems about moving out

Eli:
WTF? Was someone going to inform me of this?

@shiloh are you alright?

Spencer:
@shiloh kitten, did we do something
wrong?

Jace:
Moving?!?! I thought he was just
donating stuff

Scott:
I can't believe I'm saying this...I agree
with @Eric

Trust our kitten on this and let it go
for now

Lucky:
@Spencer you are a bad daddy! Leave
my kitty alone!He knows what he's doing

Eli:
@Lucky sweetie we trust him

We just want him to be safe

Lucky:
Like you wanted me safe last year at the
Halloween party?

Oof. As much as I appreciate Lucky standing up for
me and my independence, that is a low blow for both his
Daddy and his uncle. It was one thing for him to imply it
in front of relative strangers to the incident, but calling
them out directly is not something I expected from him.

Eric:
Accurate @Lucky

But OUCH

@Eli @Spencer are going to need something for those burns

Jay:
As entertaining as it is to see my fellow Doms get their asses handed to them by our house subs I have to pick up a pup.

Eli:
He's done with work already? He only started an hour ago.

Scott:
Does anyone know what he even does for work?

Jay:
I'm not sure but whatever his job is, I'm going to be convincing him to quit. This is too damn far away from home and school for him to be relying on rideshare.

Eli:
Where are you picking him up?

Jay:
Aspinwall

Lucky:

Wait a second... Toby's job isn't in Aspinwall. He

works by the community college and takes a bus most of the way. He only has to use rideshare to get back and forth from the university since the bus runs between the two schools. Why is he all the way out in Aspinwall?

Setting down my phone, I figure I can at least help my new roommate clear out the room while he is downstairs. First I start taking all of the boxes from the trash side down the stairs to put in the dumpster. I will start hauling the keep boxes into what I'm assuming would be the dining area, if there was a table, once I get the trash all thrown out.

I do notice that the corner gets excellent light for a big bean bag chair for kitty naps...

Nope! Not gonna scare away my new roommate who doesn't know the first thing about kitten play.

Before I can get the door open, the bottom rips out and various pieces of hockey stuff spreads over the the hardwood floor. I might not know much about hockey, but I've watched a few Pens games with the rest of the house, so I know that anything with Mario Lemieux or Sidney Crosby on it is valuable at the very least for nostalgia. I must have been confused on which pile of boxes were trash.

I hurriedly unpack one of my boxes that's just clothing and neatly repack the box of hockey stuff. The Lemieux jersey looks like it would fit Lucky, not a grown man, so I'm certain it's a special memento from his childhood. As I hold it up to get the wrinkles out and fold it, I notice there's a signature on the belly of the penguin.

I definitely got the piles mixed up. There is no chance in hell that he meant to throw away this stuff.

29

DONNIE

After locking up my office, I decide I should go upstairs and find out what Shiloh wants to do for dinner. I forgot to get his number before heading down to close up, so I should probably rectify that while I'm at it. As soon as I lock the door between the shop and the private hallway that leads back to the stairs, I feel a draft coming from somewhere.

As I clear the corner, I see the back door propped open with the two by four with a few boxes sitting inside. I hear the lid slam open on the dumpster and smile at the realization that my new roommate decided to help me haul my trash away. Picking up the closest box, I'm surprised by the weight of it.

Is this one of his?

Setting it back on the floor, I pull open the tape to see nothing but receipts.

SHIT!

I race out the back door to see Shiloh struggling to lift a box over the lip of the dumpster.

"WAIT!" I call out, but not before the box tips over the edge of the metal box and disappears into God only knows what that is inside.

Shiloh shrinks back against the bin and I am mentally kicking myself for yelling at him. I want to comfort him, but first I have to salvage whatever has already gone into the dumpster. Hoisting myself up over the edge, I can see it was only the one box, and I sigh in relief that it landed on some cardboard and not the coffee grounds that I just tossed an hour ago.

"I'm s-s-s-sorry. I was trying to b-b-be help-hel-helpful."

I drop to the ground and pull the stuttering man into my arms. Eric's warning about touching Shiloh doesn't even register in my head until well after I'm holding his trembling form. If he makes a move to want to get away from me, I'll release him immediately, but at this point, I think it's better to not make a thing out of it until he does.

"It's okay," I whisper while twirling the end of one of his braids. "I wasn't clear enough on what was trash. It's not your fault."

I feel a slight push against my chest, so I step back and release Shiloh from my embrace. I don't know what I expected to see, but it sure as shit wasn't surprise and possibly anger.

"You were going to throw away a SIGNED Mario Lemieux jersey?!"

I'm not sure why his opinion on it affects me more than everyone else who has tried to tell me that hockey isn't at fault for what happened. But the look on Shiloh's face at the thought of throwing away that jersey shames me into changing my mind a little bit. It couldn't hurt at least looking through the boxes.

After grabbing the box of Walt's terrible record keeping out of the dumpster, the only casualty of my dive seems to be my left shoe and sock. The cardboard was not as thick as I hoped and my foot went through it and into something downright foul. Instead of trying to salvage the shoe, I pulled off the left and went back inside wearing only my right sock on my feet, much to Shiloh's amusement.

Once we get all of the boxes back upstairs, I pull off the lone sock and toss it in the hamper in the bathroom. Coming out of the bathroom, I notice Shiloh staring at the corner of my little nook off the kitchen. I think Walt intended it to be a dining nook, but I've never seen a point in having a designated dining area as a single person. That's what TV trays are for.

"Whatcha looking at?" I ask him as I grab a Sprite from the fridge. "If you want to use that space for something, feel free. I was going to set up a weight bench or something there for exercise, but I would need to reinforce the floor. I won't have the funds for that any time soon."

I think I hear him say something like "kitty nook" under his breath but I can't be sure. Shaking himself out of his thoughts, he follows me onto the couch when I take a seat. I flip through the local stations to see if there's anything good on the channels I get for free with the antenna before I give up and turn on Netflix.

"What are you in the mood for?" I ask him when he just sits there quietly. "We also need to figure out food. I can cook, but I'd much rather just get something delivered at this point."

"I'm good," Shiloh says, barely above a whisper.

Fuck... I screwed up with him earlier.

Me:
How do I get him to talk?

Matt Barnes:
Shy's well shy

Treat him like you'd treat a stray cat

Me:
?????

He's a person

I can't treat him like an animal

Matt Barnes:
Remember how I told you about pet play?

Me:
So you're saying?

Matt Barnes:
Yes

Shiloh drops into kitten space after big things

Moving is a big thing

Me:
Me yelling at him probably didn't help

Matt Barnes:
I'll FUCKING GUT YOU LIKE A SARDINE YOU LIMP DICKED CUMSPOUT!

Eric stole my phone

But I second his sentiment

What the fuck did you do?

30

TOBY

I don't even wait for Jay to put the car in park before I'm racing up to our room...my room?

No! It's our room. It will be our room until I find him the perfect handler.

Throwing open the door, it looks just the same as it always does, except I don't see the kitty toys on the floor. That's fine though because Shy just picked up after himself for a change. That's all it is.

I can hear people in the hallway, but I know Jay was wrong. Shiloh wouldn't have left me like that. He wouldn't have moved out without telling me.

I open the closet to put away my bag, but Scott pushes it closed before I can.

"Toby, there's something you need to know," he says with his Dom voice. I chuckle and push his hand away from the closet door.

"Funny trick guys, but today isn't the day to pull this on me."

Spencer practically tumbles down the stairs, looking barely alive from whatever virus he has, at the same time that Eli and Jay reach our floor. Scott pulls me into the hallway gently while everyone is gathering.

"It's not funny, you guys," I stomp my foot as the looks on their faces start to scare me. "Is he hiding out over at Matt and Eric's place? At Ash's? I know I've been fucking up a lot lately, but this isn't something to joke about."

Lucky's sniffle breaks through in a way no words could. Staring at the little's face, I see the truth in his eyes.

"No... No way... He wouldn't!"

Racing to my closet, I throw open the door knowing what I'm about to see, but hoping it's not true.

Only one collar is hanging there, and it's mine.

The world around me disappears as I feel my body falling.

He really left me. I drove him away.

31

SHILOH

It's been two weeks since I moved in with Donnie, but I miss my best friend. The first night I was here, I slept on the couch. Even though Donnie said I could use his bed, I really couldn't. I might end up liking him too much and then I will have to hurt even worse when the two of them end up together. All I need to do is get Toby to come visit.

> **Me:**
> I miss my puppy

> **BFF:**
> Sorry. Working.

Throwing my phone down on my bed, I remember that this is my fault. I knew if I stayed to tell everyone face to face that I was moving, they would have talked me out of it. I never would have had the strength to walk away, to keep them safe. Seeing Toby beg me to stay would have broken me, so I asked Scott to break it to him gently before I made him drive away after dropping me off.

After that first night here, I pulled myself out of the group chat since I'm no longer living at Kink Manor. I miss my phone blowing up at all hours because of Lucky being cute or Eric being a diva or Toby's excitement over something horribly mundane.

It's too quiet here.

Even with the coffee shop downstairs, the silence is suffocating. Donnie spends his days in the shop while I hang out up here when I'm not in class or in the studio. I've tried leaving the TV on for noise, but it doesn't help. I need my best friend.

> **Me:**
> Want to come over to hang out after class?

> **Lucky:**
> Let me ask Daddy

> **Me:**
> Or maybe Spence can take us to DC?

> **Lucky:**
> OOOOOOOO
>
> I'll say pretty please
>
> That always works

The smile on my face dies as I look away from the phone toward the closet where I hid my kitten gear. I've only ever been in the playroom once without Toby. Can I handle it without my guard pup to keep others away from me?

My phone vibrates next to me and I pick it up to see what the response is.

Spencer:
I think we all need a trip to the {devil emoji}

Don says he will bring you after he's done closing up

Send me a txt to let me know when u get there

I'll leave word with Clarence if we beat u there

I shoot to my feet, clutching the phone in my hand.
DONNIE WILL TAKE ME?!
Since when is my roommate into kink?
Since when is he a member of the Devil's Club?
Does he know about me?
Flopping back on the bed, I sigh and realize I have an entire hour to worry about this before my apparently kinky roommate gets upstairs to pick me up for a trip to the BDSM club.

32

DONNIE

After the threats of dismemberment and subsequent crash course in all things kitten play that I received immediately following Shiloh becoming my roommate, Eric and Matt decided to take me their regular BDSM club, ironically named The Devil's Club. While I was getting the newbie tour from their neighbor Theo, we ran into Spencer and Lucky. It was an awkward few minutes until I told Lucky that he looked adorable and that I had a new coloring book for him at the shop whenever he might need it.

After that, everything else seemed to move along quite smoothly. The individual rooms were... let's say interesting. I'm not sure how much enjoyment I would get out of public urination or showering. I had enough of that playing hockey, and reminders of that time in my life are generally not bringing about good reactions for me.

The age play area looked like a kid's paradise. As soon

as we reached the doorway, Lucky kissed his Daddy and ran off to play. Theo chuckled while Spencer chased after his boy. Eric just smiled indulgently as if he was a doting uncle. But the next stop was a room that took my breath away—the pet room.

Watching the pups play on the obstacle course and fetch and run around was exhilarating. I knew immediately that this is the room I belong in. Even though I have no desire to run around, I know that I want to be the one to take care of the pets in this room, maybe one or two in particular.

Theo chuckled again when he led me back to the front and I filled out the paperwork. We all knew I would be back, hopefully with a kitten in tow, and if we're lucky, a pup.

Over the two weeks since then, I have been trying to figure out how to broach the subject with my roommate. I took Matt's suggestion of treating him like a cat to heart, but like his feline counterpart, Shiloh is nowhere to be found when I'm actually looking for him.

Plus, I have been thoroughly confused as to why Toby hasn't come by yet. From everything I've seen with those two, they are usually inseparable. Did Shiloh moving in with me really affect their friendship that much? Pulling out my phone, I send a message to the one person who could possibly make sense of this drama.

Me:
Did I break up Shiloh and Toby?

Diva:

It's not you D-man

Shy didn't tell him he was leaving

Me:

That's all?

Diva:

That's enough

Those 2 need each other like oxygen but T won't let it go until they see each other again

Me:

Don't they have classes together?

Diva:

Maybe at the same times

Or close enuff

But opposite ends of campus

Shy is an art major

T is business

Me:

How do we get them together then?

Even tho he hides I kno it hurts him to not see his bff

Diva:

Hang on

I have a little calling me

I put my phone to the side while I finish balancing the books for today. It wasn't a bad day, but I definitely need to do better than this if I'm going to be able to fund some renovations over the summer. I didn't find out until I did the taxes last year that Walt qualified for a shit ton of breaks that I do not, so the margin of disposable income I have is significantly less than what I was led to believe I would be working with when I drew up the plans for the expansion.

My phone ringing pulls me away from the depressive thoughts of having to push back the expansion and renovations for another year. If only I could get a loan...

"Hello?" I answer without looking at the screen. At this point, I will take any distractions I can get.

"Hey Hastings."

Only one person calls me that without condescension.

"Spencer. I just finished closing up. What's up?"

I can hear Lucky giggling in the background and I think trying to whisper, but as a little he is not very good at whispering. "Daddy is going to invite him and then you invite Toby and then we will leave them there!"

Spencer groans in my ear before muttering, "Don't suppose you can pretend you didn't hear that?"

I chuckle at the absurdity that my life has become, but listen to the proposal they came up with for getting the two best friends to work their shit out.

"Sounds like a plan," I tell him as I stretch my arms above my head. "If you want Shiloh to have a chance to process it before I get upstairs, you should let him know

now. I have about ten minutes worth of cleanup and then I'll grab him to head over."

"Why does he need time to process?" Spencer asks before I can end the call.

"Because I haven't been able to tell him I joined the DC yet," I tell him and press the end call button. Throwing the door closed on the safe, I start laughing to myself, imagining how my kitten... erm Shiloh will take the news.

33
SHILOH

I didn't mean to hit Donnie in the face with my plug tail, honest. He just surprised me when I was digging through my box of gear to decide what was appropriate to have my new sexy roommate see me in at the club for the first time. I wasn't even going to use that one! I only bought it to work up the courage to try and get Toby to see me as more, but I really am a scaredy cat.

"For the last time, Shiloh, I'm fine. It's not even swelling up," Donnie says from the seat next to me. After I heard the thunk, I slid myself under the bed until I saw his feet leave the room, but when I looked, half of my gear and my bag were gone, including the plug tail...

"O-okay," I manage to get out as we pull into the parking lot of the club. Before I can get it myself, Donnie grabs my bag out of the backseat and heads for the front doors of the club.

Oh, fuck a duck, this is going to be embarrassing.

I barely manage to catch up before I hear Clarence's voice ring through the lobby area.

"Who did *you* get into a fight with?"

By pure reflex, I start gathering my braids in front of my face to hide. There's nowhere to disappear in the lobby and I have to check in before I can let myself go into kitty space. I'm so distracted by trying to hide that Clarence has to call out to me a few times to get my attention.

"Hey, kitty cat," he croons when he sees he finally has my attention. "Ready to get checked in so you can claim your nap spot?"

I can feel myself starting to sink further into that more animalistic headspace with every second I'm in the building, so I nod and pull out my wallet so that Clarence can swipe my ID card and let us through. The beep and green light is always my brain's signal that it's safe to relax and I feel myself drift a little further away from being human.

"Do you want my help getting changed?" the man next to asks... Donnie. I almost forgot who I was here with. Wait. There was something I was supposed to do before going back....

"I'll let them know you're here, sweetie," Clarence says from behind us. "Don't worry about it and go ahead and enjoy yourselves."

Donnie leads me to a private changing room instead of the group rooms. I don't understand why he's worried about changing in public. He played sports all the way through college according to Eric.

"I don't need a private room. I'm fine with changing in front of the other people here," I tell him, hoping he can get his money back for reserving a private room. "Anything I don't want to share with everyone else, I just use a stall."

My shorts can be a little difficult to put on, especially with threading my tail through the hole in the ass. I bought them hoping to push me into wearing the plug, but I can't bring myself to put my fingers there to prep enough to get the plug in.

"The room is for me, kitty cat," he tells me with a soft pat on the top of my head. "Group changing and shower type areas bring up memories I would much rather keep buried for the time being."

Oh.

Is it wrong that I'm a little disappointed that this special room *isn't* for me?

Damnit, Shiloh! You're supposed to be getting him together with Toby!

Giving him a nod, I set my bag down and start pulling out everything so that I can get changed... Ignoring the plug...

He seemed to grab everything I need except – there's no other tail but the plug.

34

DONNIE

Despite the need to explain my reserving a private changing room, I am thoroughly excited to experience the pet area with my kitten... erm Shiloh. I don't need to change into anything, but I pull off my hoodie, socks, and shoes to be fully comfortable for some kitty snuggles if he wants them. While he's distracted searching his bag for his other tail, I pull the kitten and puppy treats out of my bag and stuff them in my back pockets.

Lucky bounced into the shop last week with his thumb in his mouth and thrust an index card at me before skipping back out the door. I got a quick wave from Spencer before I looked down and saw a recipe for some apple cinnamon and peanut butter banana treats along with a recommendation to use cookie cutters to differentiate between the two. The apple cinnamon were labeled kitten treats and the peanut butter banana were puppy treats.

I ended up taking a morning off while Shiloh was

doing his studio time this week to make them and have time to clean up and air out the apartment. I want them to be a surprise for the both of them.

"Um, Donnie?" Shiloh looks up at me as he drops his now empty bag to the floor. "I think you forgot to pack my tail."

Reaching into my bag, I pull out a small bottle of lube and hold it out to him. "I figured since you have the plug tail and the shorts you do that you only use the plug one. I didn't see any lube in your stuff so I grabbed a bottle from my room."

Shiloh takes the lube from my hand like it's a dangerous animal and picks up his tail gingerly with the other hand. The confusion on his face doesn't make sense, unless...

"Have you ever used the plug, Shiloh?"

He glances up at me before his arms drop to his sides and he shakes his head. The sadness radiating off of him is not what I had expected when I packed for him. He was supposed to be shy, but then we'd go have some fun after he got over his embarrassment. I mean, he got over giving me a shiner with the damn thing.

"I can't be kitty without a tail," he says in a strained voice, and I feel like absolute dogshit for not grabbing the other one as well.

"I'm so sorry, kitten," I tell him and start to pull my shoes back on my feet. "I'll run back home and get your other one. I didn't know you needed that one instead of the plug."

My arms are in the sleeves of my hoodie and I'm

about to pull it over my head when I feel a hand on my bicep. I look over at the shy boy who is stealing more of my heart every day and see a light in his eyes that has been missing for the last two weeks.

"Maybe you can help me? I've never... I don't know how to..."

Oh, fuck me...

This boy is going to be the death of me.

Plucking the lube and tail from his hands, I tell him to get ready and we'll do his tail last. After all, that's the reason his shorts are the way they are.

Kicking off my shoes again, I'm transfixed watching the shy man in front of me transform with each piece of gear he puts on. The only thing he hesitates with is his collar. With a sad sigh, he places it back in the bag and zips it up.

"I'm ready."

Lord, I wish I was. My stomach is nothing but knots as I position him bent over the back of the couch in the room. Kneeling down behind him, I can't help but groan at the sight of him. I don't know how he does it, but somehow the little shit purrs in response, giving his hips a little wiggle. I grab his hips to hold him still before I move my hands to the opening in his shorts to separate his cheeks to make sure everything is lined up correctly.

That flash of pink in the center of all of that mocha rips another sound from my chest, but it was too guttural, too primal to be a mere groan. It was a sound of pure need, pure possession. There's a part of me that is beyond elated to be the first to breach him there, even if it is only my fingers tonight.

As much as I want a taste, I know that the rest of the guys will be showing up soon with Toby, and I want Shiloh to be fully kitten by that point. So my hunger is put on the back burner while I lube up two fingers to open my kitten up for his tail.

"Mrow?" Shiloh squeaks in curious surprise as I push into him before he relaxes into the feeling. I'm thinking the plug tail is going to become his favorite tail after tonight.

35

TOBY

"Get in, pup," Jay calls out to me and I almost drop my phone in surprise. After the whole fainting thing a couple of weeks ago, I had to come clean to my housemates about why I was in Aspinwall and why I lied to them. I knew they would understand, but I didn't want to risk them treating me differently for having so much anger inside of me.

"I was gonna call," I tell him defiantly as I climb into the passenger seat of his car. I totally wasn't going to call. Doctor Monroe opened my eyes to some things today that I didn't want to look too closely at, and I was hoping for a long ass ride with a stranger to sort through it all.

"Too bad," Jay says as he heads toward home. "House trip to DC tonight and your presence is mandatory."

My breath hitches. I can't go to the club without Shiloh. I've never been in there without him. Part of my being safe as a pup is knowing he is there and that I'm there for him. It's not the same without him.

"I can't," I whisper as I stare out the window. Jay turns down the music and glances at me while he fights to change lanes so we don't get stuck going through the tunnel.

"What do you mean? Do you have work tonight or something?"

I shake my head before resting my forehead on the cool glass. The leaves have really decided to change colors over the last week or so and I guess it's pretty, especially with the reflection in the river.

"Talk to me, pup. Why can't you come out with us?" Jay demands in his Daddy voice. He doesn't usually pull that out on us, so I to react to it without thinking.

"I can't be a pup without my kitten," I say as the first tear drips onto the door. "I've never been there without Shiloh, but he left me. He doesn't need me anymore. What good am I if he doesn't need me as his guard dog anymore?"

Jay drives along in silence for a little while until the gas light comes on and he decides to pull in for gas at the Sheetz instead of hitting up our usual spot for gas five minutes up the road. I try to let the heavy metal rile me up, but there's nothing left inside of me.

"... not gonna work, Spencer! He won't be able to reach pupspace. Not today... I understand they're already there, but I can't in good conscience... Fucker, he's crying! The fucking thought of going in there brought him to tears!... I won't... don't you dare put him...*Hey* Lucky..."

I don't like Daddy Jay being angry. And just like everything else, it's my fault. I sniffle and wipe at my eyes to try and push the sads back down again. It's all because of what Doctor Monroe said today. She's wrong, of course. I'm not missing my mother. I'm missing my best friend who doesn't need me anymore.

"... okay little one... yes, I will... I'll tell him... okay, Lucky. Put your Daddy back on the phone please... That was low even for you, ya fucking jagoff... Yeah, we're coming."

Jay puts the nozzle back and grabs his receipt before he gets back in the car. When we pull out onto the road, he glances at me with worry in his eyes.

"I tried to get you out of it, Pup, but Lucky has his heart set on everyone being there tonight. If you still want to ditch after seeing him, I'll take you right home, I promise."

Leaning my forehead back against the cool window, I sigh. This is my new normal, I guess. I need to get used to life without my Shiloh.

36

TOBY

"The guys already took your gear in," Clarence tells me as the light turns green when he swipes my ID. "They didn't want anyone to mess with it, so it's in private room number three. Code for the door is your birthday, sweetie."

I don't know what my face is showing, but it's obvious I'm not doing a very good job of hiding my feelings. I don't want to be here without my kitten. My inner pup doesn't want to play. He just wants to howl and whine and beg for his kitten to come back to him.

"Do you need help getting into your gear?" Jay asks when we reach the door for room three. "I know Shiloh usually helped, but I can help with the buckles and everything tonight."

I can't stop the whimper that escapes at the realization that I can't even go full pup without help anymore. I mean, the jock and the plug tail I can do by myself... same with the pads and the leg straps. But if I'm by myself, I have to choose between the mits and the hood. It's been over a year since I've been without either.

Looking up at Jay, I see the pity in his eyes. I'm pathetic...

"I got you, Toby," he says softly as he opens the door to reveal my bag sitting on a couch. There's a bead on the floor that looks a bit like the ones I helped Shiloh put in his hair and it sets off another whimper. As the door closes, Jay pulls me into his chest and the floodgates open.

"Let it all out, pup. Let it out."

I don't know how long I cried for, but Daddy Jay's shirt is soaked through when I pull back and he hands me a water.

"Hydrate first, then get changed with what you can do yourself. I'll be back once I grab my stuff from my lock box."

Being alone in the changing room is heavier than anything else I've ever felt.

You're afraid of losing people just like you lost your mother, Tobias.

Shut up, Doctor Monroe!

Yanking open the zipper on my bag of gear, I start pulling everything out only to realize I forgot to put a new bottle of lube in there after running out last time we were here. In the main changing area, there's almost always someone there with lube in a pinch, but I've never been in a private room to see what they stock.

Fuck it. I'll get everything else on and borrow some from Jay's diaper bag when he gets back. He's definitely an overly prepared Daddy.

I finish getting everything I can on and move my bag to the low table in front of the couch. Glancing around the room, it looks like it's set up to be like a dorm or cheap apartment type of vibe. I can dig it in a way. I would definitely be more comfortable doing something in here compared to say the classroom set-up in room seven.

Jay is taking forever to grab his diaper bag, so I can only assume he came across a boy or girl needing his help. He might be homosexual, but he will be a Daddy to absolutely anybody who needs one. I really hope he can find his boy someday soon.

Out of boredom, I throw myself down on the couch and yelp as something cold and hard presses on my left asscheek. Leaning over, I dig my hand between the cushions to feel for whatever it was that poked me. My fingers brush against something hard and plastic and I pull it out in triumph.

LUBE!

I don't know what gods are looking down on me today, but at least now I won't have to suffer trying to rush through inserting my tail with Jay in the room. The man is like a brother to me. It would be awkward with a capital A for him to watch me fingering my hole.

My tail gets placed on the cushion nest to me as I kneel facing the back of the couch to get a good angle for doing this. Usually in the main changing room, I do this in a stall so that I don't make Shiloh nervous or give anyone any ideas. I'm not exactly shy, but I'm not into voyeurism.

Two lubed fingers go in and I have to remind myself that this is just stretching. I'm not looking to get off. I just need to get my tail in so that Jay can help me with my mitts and my hood...

The sound of the door opening has me pausing. Fuck.

"Just give me a minute, Jay. I'm almost ready for you," I call out as I scissor my fingers faster, trying to get open enough to where I can shove the tail in without worrying about tearing.

"Jay got held up."

37

DONNIE

When Jay finds me in the pet room, he hurries to explain what is going on with Toby and asks me to go explain things to him. The look in Jay's eyes tells me that there is something really wrong with Toby today, and I have an urgent need to fix it.

"I'll sit with the kitten," he says as he pushes me toward my private room. "We stuck him in your room so that you can have this talk without worrying about nebby assholes."

I turn back to look at Shiloh sprawled out on a beanbag chair in the corner of the room, eyes tracking all of the pups running around.

"I've got him," Jay hisses at me. "Go now before he notices you leaving. He's fine as long as one of us is here, but he tries to follow if he sees one of us leaving the room. I don't have the skillset to deal with trying to herd a cat tonight."

After seeing Shiloh fully embrace being a cat for the

last twenty minutes or so, I can't help but huff a laugh at the image of Jay trying to wrangle Shiloh. The boy may be skinny, but he is very wiggly and flexible as a kitten.

The smile freezes on my face when I open the door to my changing room and see Toby shove three fingers into his hole and announce that he's "almost ready" for another man. The front part of my brain realizes that Jay told Toby that he was coming back to help him with his gear. The dumbass primitive lizard brain of mine doesn't come close to thinking of that.

"Jay got held up," I say with a growl to my voice. I've gone back to that caveman state I was in while helping Shiloh insert his tail. No one but me is going to be putting anything in this man's ass.

Toby squeals and flails around at the sound of my voice. I barely manage to catch him before he crashes through the coffee table behind him. Propping him back up, I grab the bottle of lube laying on the couch next to him, smirking at the fact that he is using my bottle, and lube up my fingers in anticipation of assisting my pup in the same way I did our kitten earlier.

"Need some help, Pup?"

The needy whine that escapes his throat is replaced by spitting when he slaps his hands over his mouth, including his lube soaked fingers.

Yeah. Regular lube does not taste very good.

"I usually do this part by myself," he manages to get out after wiping his mouth, face, and hands with the towel I hand him from my bag. "I was waiting on Jay to help with my mitts and hood since I can't do them both by myself."

Nodding, I slide my slicked up fingers through his crack and lean over him to whisper in his ear. "Are you sure you only want help with those?"

The whine comes out again, but this time Toby just looks at me with the most perfect case of puppy dog eyes I've ever come across.

"Words, pup," I tell him with a little smack to his left asscheek. "Until that hood goes on, I need words from you. Am I giving you your tail or do you want to do it?"

"You," he manages to whimper and I slide two fingers in easily. Where Shiloh was obviously unaccustomed to anything being inserted, Toby is the opposite. He is relishing every twitch and curl of my fingers as I loosen him up. In no time at all, I'm able to insert a third which causes Toby to howl and collapse against the back of the couch.

"That's it, pup. Let me in."

The needy sounds coming from Toby's throat are most definitely affecting me, but I'm nog going to be taking my own pleasure in this room. That has to wait for the two friends to reconcile. I refuse to come between them.

Leaning around the man in front of me, I see a wet spot forming on the front of his jock, barely visible through the black fabric. With the hand not inserted in his ass, I pull down the fabric and release his dick to the cooler air in the room.

"Please?" Toby whines and those baby blues hit me like a bolt of lightning. "I need..."

"I know what you need."

Grasping his cock, I stroke him in tandem with my fingers going in and out of his hole. The sounds coming from the pup push me higher and higher, but I know I have to hold back.

In an effort to stop myself from cumming in my pants, I start kissing along the top of Toby's back. The way his cries pitch higher and his body tenses tells me he's very close now.

Three more strokes and his hole clamps down on my fingers with a pressure that has my dick threatening to rip through my jeans. Instinctively, I bite down to prevent myself from making a mess in my boxer briefs.

I forgot that Toby was the one I was biting until his pleasured squeal registers in my ears. Hurriedly, I release him from my mouth and pull off of him, leaving him to collapse boneless against the back of the couch. The look on his face tells me he is anything but unhappy with the result, but I need to wait for the endorphins to fade a bit before I fully make that assumption.

"Ready for your tail, Pup?" I ask when his brain appears to come back online.

Licking his lips, Toby nods emphatically.

I'm so going to end up spoiling these boys.

38

SHILOH

There is something in my ass. There is something in my ass. There is something in my ass.

As much as I try to ignore it, every time I shift on my napping cushion, I feel the plug shift inside of me. It wasn't so bad when Donnie was there to look at and remember how it felt when he put it in, but Jay is here and Donnie went somewhere.

And these pups in the room are too violent. They're too pushy. I don't want to play with them. I don't want them near me. They aren't Toby.

A ball rolls near my cushion and a burly pup comes barrelling toward me. Human Shiloh would run, but me as a kitty? I brace myself up on my fingers and toes and hiss at the intrusion to my lassitude. The offensive pup actually has the audacity to growl at me?

Does he not realize I am a cat and therefore superior?

Only one pup is on my level and this bitch is not it.

I hiss at him again, arching my back higher. However,

he stalks forward with a growl, hurt is in his eyes. He's like Michael. He's more than a sadist. He's a predator.

I let out a loud yowl followed by a third hiss as I back up against the wall. Fuck me, I let myself get cornered. My eyes dart around the room, but only the other pups are looking. A few look conflicted, but the closest ones look to be ready to jump in to help my attacker.

Where the fuck is Jay? I locate him across the room, tending to an injured pup by the obstacle course.

Of fucking course he is. I can't even be mad at him for that. Fucking Daddies...

The growl in front of me is closer and the pup starts running for me, realizing that no one is going to stop him and he can explain it away as rough play.

Toby, I'm sorry.

The second before the bastard makes contact, I curl up into as small of a ball as I can make my body. I know this is going to hurt... But I feel no pain. Was he just messing with me?

I open my eyes to see my attacker feet away, clutching his side and howling in pain. Blocking his path to me is none other than the man I've needed to see for the last two weeks. Even after everything I put him through, he still defended me.

"Easy, Pup."

I look toward the door and see Donnie heading toward us both. As soon as he reaches me, he leans down to run his hand from the top of my head down to my tail, giving it a small tug.

"You can relax, Kitty Cat. I'm back now. I had to go wrangle our pup."

Toby turns back to us at the sound of Donnie's voice and the look in his eyes makes me feel like absolute shit. He's asking *me* for forgiveness when I was the one who fucked everything up. I don't deserve him, but fuck if I'm not going to do everything I can to make him the happiest man on the planet... him and Donnie.

Crawling over to him, I rub my body along his side, like I've done hundreds of times before. It's my request to cuddle when I'm in kittyspace, and Toby knows it. His soft yip tells me all is forgiven and he plops himself down on my cushion, wiggling on his back in an effort to get belly rubs from our Donnie.

I wind myself around Donnie's legs to encourage him to join us before I curl in next to my best friend and hope that this peace of ours lasts.

39

DONNIE

Coming out of the changing room with Toby in full pup mode is an experience. As soon as the mitts and hood went on, he became a dog. I thought it would be hard to differentiate between the human and the pet, but these two men make it very easy to know when to treat them as their animal personas or their human sides. From what I've read online, it usually takes a lot of trust for a sub in pet play to let go like they do.

A strange sound from the direction of the pet room niggles at the back of my mind, and I feel the need to run to the room. Apparently, Toby feels the same as he takes off, moving much faster than I ever imagined considering how his legs are restrained. I would not like to be his knees in the morning.

By the time I catch up to him and enter the pet room, I see chaos in the corner where Shiloh had set himself up. Taking in the scene, I feel my blood start to boil. My kitten is shaking and backed completely into the corner.

Toby has taken up a protective stance in front of Shiloh, growling at a much bigger pup who is on the floor, swearing and grunting in pain.

Jay rushes over to the man writhing on the ground and looks like he's going to admonish my pup until he glances back at the kitten against the wall.

Where the fuck was Jay, anyway?

Where the fuck are the monitors that are supposed to be in the play rooms?

I take a few minutes to comfort my boys and settle them onto the cushion to cuddle for a bit. Now that I know things are good between them, at least so far as Toby will protect Shiloh if I step away, I need to get some answers.

"Toby?" I drag him from his half doze with a bit of a belly rub. The way his leg twitches like a real dog's would makes me chuckle. "I'm going to find out what the fuck happened in here and make sure it doesn't happen again. Can you be a good boy and protect our kitten while I'm out?"

He whimpers a bit when he sees Jay by the door, but then meets my eye and gives a soft woof so as not to disturb the napping kitten curled into his side. I know he won't let anyone hurt Shiloh, but something tells me he needs to be reminded of that after the display of aggression.

As soon as I meet Jay at the door, I grab his arm and drag him toward the front room where I know we'll find Theo or someone who can get me whoever is in charge of the monitors for the rooms.

"Look Don, I'm sorry," Jay says as soon as we're in the hallway. "There was an injury and I can't ignore that. I tried, but there was no one else around to help. No one had even attempted to approach Shy, so I figured a few minutes wouldn't be an issue."

I turned on him and backed him into the wall. He might be the same height as me, but I have a lifetime of hockey conditioning behind me. I'm stronger than I look.

"Fuck that!" I hiss. "That pup wanted to hurt someone smaller and weaker than him. I'm pretty sure if they review the footage, that pup also hurt the one you were tending to in order to get you over to the other side of the room. They targeted *my* kitten and they will pay for that."

"Cyril goes by he/him, but I doubt you're wrong," Clarence says when he comes up to us. "Let's take this in the office and I can review the tapes. If Cyril did injure another member, he will be banned."

Swallowing my anger, I release Jay so that we can follow Clarence into the unlabeled room in the middle of the hallway. If it wasn't for the handle, you wouldn't even notice the door in the dim light.

Sitting down at the computer, Clarence turns the monitor to the side so that we can all see. As the footage goes, there is no sound, but that is typical in Pennsylvania. It is an all party consent state for audio recordings, so it's usually easier for businesses to only have visual. Considering the audio doesn't matter in this instance, I'm not worried about it.

We started watching the feed from the moment

Shiloh and I entered the room. I can't hide the smirk on my face when Shiloh sits on the cushion and pops right back up, staring at his ass in wonder.

"Well that's a happy kitty," Clarence chuckles as he adjusts the camera to zoom in on Cyril and some other pups.

"And there it is," he sighs. "The pack watched him from the moment he came in. They set it up."

"They?" Jay asks. "I thought it was all Cyril. I mean he's a pompous ass outside of here, so his behavior doesn't really surprise me. But who else was it?"

Clarence zooms in on the screen where it shows them all talking, which should be a red flag to begin with. The pup who was injured breaks away from the group and we watch as Jay runs away from Shiloh to help.

"Where was the monitor?" I ask when Clarence switches back to the live feed and I see my boys content in their corner with a few pups randomly walking past. Toby doesn't react to them, so I assume they are harmless.

Clarence rubs his temples and gives us a look as if he's a single mother raising triplets.

"Theo found him balls deep in some random chick in room seven. She isn't even a member, but he snuck her in the back entrance," he says through gritted teeth. "Tom has never been irresponsible, but from the look in his eyes, I think he got involved in drugs or something. He is definitely high tonight, and the girl was barely cognizant, let alone sober enough for consent.

"That is the kind of shit that will get us shut down if the wrong cops are called or the wrong judge gets the case. So I called in a couple members who are on the force and sent an email to Alex to see if we can get a sympathetic judge."

I feel for Clarence. Really, I do. But I don't give a fuck about the club right now. Shiloh was attacked, premeditated, and so far all I'm seeing is nothing.

40

SHILOH

I'm not sure how long I was snoozing, curled up against Toby's side in our corner of the play room, but Donnie's hand on my side brings me back to awareness. With a short purr and a headbutt to his palm, he takes the hint and gives me scritches behind my ear and under my chin.

"Time to head home, Kitten," he says as he stands back up. "You've both got class in the morning and I have a coffee shop to run."

Toby's whine makes me grumble out a noise I've never made before. It shocks all three of us until Donnie starts belly laughing.

I like that sound. I want to hear more of it.

"Come on boys. Let's get you back to being people so we can go home."

Toby follows like the obedient pup he is, and I follow because I want to. A cat chooses their person, after all...

Shit.

I let Donnie become my person. He's supposed to be

Toby's person, not mine. I don't need a person. People hurt people who look like me, and I'm so tired of being hurt.

As the door closes to our changing room, I notice that Toby's gear bag is already in here with us. How did that happen?

Fuck it. It doesn't matter.

While Donnie pulls off Toby's hood and gives him the love and pets that I used to do, I grab the bag with my regular clothes and head for the small half bath that is in the room. I need to let them have their moment. This is what I wanted after all, right?

As soon as the door is closed between us, my ass hits the floor, pushing the tail plug against my prostate in a way it's been teasing all night but never quite hitting until this moment. I can't stop the sound that escapes but at this point it's more pain than pleasure. My body absolutely loves it, but my heart shatters.

"Kitten, you alright?" Donnie's voice comes from the other side of the door.

"MmmHmm," I make an affirmative noise to try and get him to stay out. If I were to use words, he would hear it. He would know how I feel. If he knows how I feel, he will either move me out or reject Toby for me. I can't be selfish. Toby needs him more.

"Shy?" Toby's voice calls out. "Shy, I'm sorry. Please don't be mad at me anymore. Please don't let me go, too."

I shove my fist into my mouth to muffle the sobs invoked by his painful words. The pain of my teeth cutting into my knuckles helps me calm down enough to sound somewhat normal when I answer.

"It's fine, Tobe. I'm not mad. I just have to pee."

I hear footsteps shuffling away from the door as I curl myself around the base of the toilet. There's not much room in here, but I'm used to squeezing into small spaces. Reaching around behind me, I pull my tail forward and let the soft texture flow through my hands. I have to pull it out...

I felt confident wearing the plug with Donnie's help, but now I have to learn to do this on my own. Gliding my hands up the length of my tail, I find the solid base of the plug and twist it to make sure there is still enough lubrication to pull it out easily. I know better than to just yank it, but I fucking want it out of me. It's nothing more than a reminder of what I'm losing tonight, what I never should have let myself take in the first place.

The pleasure of the stretch mingles with the pain of my heart breaking until I'm a sobbing mess on the tiles, the plug glistening next to me.

41

TOBY

The soft click of a door snaps me completely out of pup space as hot coffee shop owner guy starts taking off my mitts. I look around the room and panic starts to kick in. Where is Shiloh? Where did he go?

I guess my body has taken over for a second because strong arms wrap around me to hold me still.

"I'll check on him, Pup. Just go ahead and get your other mitt off and finish getting changed."

I rush through pulling off the rest of my kit and throw it haphazardly into my bag. The only things left are my tail and my jock, but I can't wait any longer.

Waddling over to the door, I'm trying to extract my tail from my ass at the same time as I'm begging my best friend to not leave me. Fuck what I said before. Doctor Monroe is right. I am terrified of losing Shiloh the same way I lost my mother. What if he wakes up one day and doesn't love me anymore?

"I'm fine, Tobe," Shiloh's soft voice carries through the door.

He's not fine.

I look at coffee shop guy. Damn, I should really remember his name. He gives me a look of concern before he pats me on the head and steps over to the landline phone on the wall of the room.

Shiloh said he needed to pee, but I don't hear it. All I hear is the sounds that would wake me up in the middle of the night. My best friend is in pain and trying to hide it from me.

Fuck it. I'm breaking down the door.

Stepping back, I get in position to ram it when a hand comes down on my shoulder.

"Theo is coming with the key, Toby. He'll be alright."

The look in his eyes is just as tortured as I'm sure mine are. Has he been cuddling Shiloh back to sleep when the nightmares hit?

Part of me is jealous that he gets to hold my kitten, but a much bigger part of me is relieved to know that Shiloh has someone big and strong to protect him and look after him.

"I tried so hard," I mumble as I fall to my knees. "Why am I never good enough?"

Shiloh's gasp of pain has me jumping to my feet, but Theo rushes into our room with Clarence and the master key for the bathroom. I'm being held back by the arms of the man I am giving my best friend to when the door opens and I howl out my pain.

42

DONNIE

Something is really wrong between these two. From the moment we got back to the changing room, the mood shifted, and I'm struggling to figure out what it is. Helping Toby get his gear off seems to be the priority for getting us ready to go home, so I work on pulling off his hood first.

"There you are, Toby," I say as I ruffle his blond mop of sweat dampened hair. I can't help but lean over and give him a kiss on his sweaty forehead for being such a good pup tonight.

While I'm removing the first mitt, I notice Shiloh slink off into the little half bath in the room. The snick of the lock doesn't surprise me, not that much. I figure he wants some privacy for removing his tail since he didn't have an audience when I helped him put it in. Then again, he's never not acknowledged if I needed the bathroom before he would occupy it at home.

Toby seems to sense something and tries to move

toward the door before he has his legs unbound and I have to keep him from faceplanting into the coffee table.

Instead of our pup killing himself in his rush to get to the door, I head over to check on Shiloh. He doesn't give me words, but the sound of his voice has me struggling to not break down the door.

Even his response to Toby makes my fear ratchet higher, despite the strange waddle maneuver our pup is doing to work the tail plug out of his ass while he's pacing in front of the bathroom door.

That's it. I'm calling for backup. This fucking club has failed Shiloh too many times tonight. A locked door is not going to stop me from helping him.

I grab the wall phone and Clarence's crisp voice comes on the line.

"Need supplies, Donald?"

"I need the fucking bathroom key. Shiloh has locked himself in and Toby is ready to break down the door. Honestly I'm inclined to let him if it wouldn't hurt him."

"Shit!" There's sounds of drawers opening followed by keys jangling. "Theo! Room three! It's our kitten!"

The line goes dead and I grab onto Toby before he finishes lining up to break down the door. I don't know if he hears me when I tell him help is on the way, but we both freeze at the sight in front of us when the door opens.

I don't know what is louder; Toby's howl of anguish or the shattering of my heart. If it wasn't for the hiccuping breaths, I would think Shiloh was dead with how he is laid out on the floor. My brain flashes back to the vision of Eric on that bed, struggling to breathe through the vomit and semen in his throat.

Toby falls to his knees when I release him and run to the trash can in the corner to vomit whatever is in my stomach. I know they need me. My boys need me, but I'm trapped in that fucking party house. I failed. I couldn't stop them. I couldn't save him.

"... Hastings? Dude, snap out of it...."

Words float by while I'm trapped in the past.

Look at that, fairy boy is choking on our cum.
        I'd rather he choke on my dick.
        Fucking faggot is begging for it.

"DON!"

A sharp pain on my cheek makes my body react and I jump to my feet to beat the shit out of someone. Never again!

"Wake the fuck up, Hastings!" Spencer says as my eyes refocus on the present. He and Eric are both in front of me with the latter shaking out his hand as if he hurt it somehow.

"You with us?" Matt calls from the direction of the couch and I nod, not trusting myself not to spew again.

Eric pushes my shoulder before sauntering over to where his boyfriend is. "Good because I am not slapping you again. What the fuck is your cheekbone made out of, concrete?"

Looking at the couch, I see Shiloh laid out, covered in a plush blanket with Toby kneeling beside his head, stroking his hand down our kitten's body, petting him to keep himself calm.

"Do we need an ambulance?" Clarence asks as the door to the room cracks open.

Matt meets him at the door shaking his head. "I got this, C. We'll go out the back tonight, though. I don't think Shy is going to be up for walking through the lounge."

Turning away from the door, Matt levels me with a glare.

"We need to talk."

43

DONNIE

"How much do you know about Shiloh's or Toby's pasts?" he asks me as he lights up a smoke as soon as we are out back.

"Nothing really. Just that Shy has that restraining order," I tell him as I try to stay upwind. "I thought you quit?"

Matt huffs his annoyance at my question. "Try living with Eric and not having something that gives you a reason to step away occasionally. *My* tolerance for his antics is endless, but I have to step away from people who don't understand him or give him weird looks. If the options are take a smoke break or knock a motherfucker out and lose my job? I'll risk the cancer."

"Bet your mom loves that."

Matt blows his smoke directly in my face, making me hack and gag... reminding me that I still haven't washed away the taste of vomit from my mouth.

"Ma doesn't know, nor will she. But back to the

matter at hand. You need to know their stories to avoid situations like tonight."

Matt finishes his smoke and pulls out some mints. I gladly take one when he offers. I figure we are going to head back in, but instead he just sits down on the bench like we'll be waiting here for them to come out.

"Long story short is both of those boys have intimacy and self esteem issues out the wazoo in addition to sporting an overly inflated martyr complex. You always have to look below the surface with those two. They could wreck the Titanic a hundred times over with the shit they keep buried, and keep in mind I've known them less than a year.

"Even my boy won't tell me details of their stories. But what I know is Toby was sent to a conversion camp by his mother when he came out to her, and Shiloh watched his mother die in front of him when he was seven years old. The man he was sent to live with after is the same one he has the restraining order against now. That's all I know."

My mind is short circuiting on the information my friend just gave me in such a nonchalant manner.

Toby, sweet playful energetic Toby, was sent to a conversion camp?

Shiloh *watched* his mother...

"I think I'm gonna be sick again," I mutter as I lean against the wall of the building.

Matt's warm hand lands in the middle of my upper back, offering me a small bit of comfort.

"You can't fall apart on them, for them. They're two

incredibly strong men who neither need nor want pity. They just want someone to *be* there, to be theirs. They don't need your strength or for you to fight their demons. They just need you."

Matt pulls me upright and turns me to face him. "You need to be willing to let them inside that head of yours and let them help you through your issues with my boy."

I pull out of his arms forcefully and almost land on my ass for my trouble.

"I don't have a problem with Eric. He's one of my best friends."

Matt shakes his head and sits back on the bench.

"One of your only friends, you mean. You've been punishing yourself for almost six years now, Don. You didn't fail him. You were almost killed trying to stop them."

"Yeah well maybe they should have just finished me off that night," I spit at him before my brain registers that the backdoor is open and the guys from Kink Manor are filing out, including Toby and Shiloh.

Fuck.

44

SHILOH

Waking up on the couch in the changing room was a bit disorienting, but the worst part has to be the looks of fear and pity on the faces of all of my friends and family who are crowded into this tiny ass room. Fucking brilliant.

"You alright, Kitty Cat?"

Eric's voice pulls my attention away from the sniffly pup still petting the top of my head. The drag queen looks like he's been put through the ringer tonight which for him can be a very good thing. He and Matt have branched out into some heavier impact play and bondage scenes as their relationship progresses.

I envy them.

"Shy-Shy?"

Lucky pokes his head around the side of his Daddy and I notice he's been crying as well.

"I'm okay, Lucky. Just some bad thoughts got too loud."

Sniffling, the little nods at me and reaches up for his Daddy to pick him up. Spencer is fortunate that his boy is honestly the size of most twelve year old boys because I couldn't imagine anyone ever denying someone as adorable as Lucky when he wants to be carried. Daddy Spence holds him like he is the greatest treasure in the world, which to be honest, he kind of is.

I envy them, too.

"Please don't let go, Shy," Toby whispers from beside me. "I want you to have him and be happy, but please don't leave me behind. Don't push me out just because we don't fit anymore. I'll change. I'll be whatever you want me to be."

Throwing off the blanket that someone draped over me, I forcefully grab Toby and pull him up on the couch with me.

"Don't you *dare* say that!," I sneer at the thought of Toby, *my Toby*, being someone other than the magnificent man that he is. "Whether we are together or on the other side of the world from each other, you need to promise me you won't change. I love you just how you are, my crazy pup. I couldn't live with myself if you changed for me."

Eric meets my eyes as I notice him ushering everyone else out of the room. He mouths the words 'back door' so that I know where to meet them once I have our excitable pup calmed down again.

"But you don't need me now that you have hot coffee shop guy. He can protect you so much better than I can. He can provide for you and keep you safe and doesn't fly off the handle because of his mommy issues."

I push Toby off of me so that I can sit up. I'm blinking rapidly trying to get my brain to make sense of the jumble of words that just came out of his mouth. Toby opens his mouth to continue his rambling, but I hold up my hand to stop him.

One thing at a time. That's the only way to tackle this.

"Hot coffee shop guy? Do you mean Donnie?"

Toby nods his head enthusiastically and sighs, "I know I was introduced ages ago, but his name kept slipping out of my head. He's perfect for you, Shy. And I know you love him, too. You wore the plug tonight."

Oh, sweet naïve silly Toby...

"I wore the plug tonight because I accidentally smacked him in the face with it when I was pulling out stuff to pack my bag for tonight. I've had it for months now, waiting for the opportunity to ask *you* to help me with it. Donnie only helped me tonight because he didn't know I had another tail and only packed the plug.

"You know I can't go full kitty without a tail to run my paws over."

Toby giggles and falls off the couch trying to hold back a full blown belly laugh.

"He got hit in the face with a butt plug?"

Aaaand there he goes.

I smile as my best friend seems to have forgotten his own insecurities for the moment. I just hope they stay buried at least until I can get him to our apartment and can show him that he's wrong about me an Donnie, even though I desperately wish it could be true.

"Let's finish getting changed and we can go meet up with everyone. I'm sure Donnie won't mind if you spend the night at our place above the shop tonight. I don't want to let you go at all, my sweet southern pup."

Toby rushes to whip off his jock and I shake my head as I slip my legs into my jeans and he puts the jock back on before pulling on his own pair of jeans. I chuckle at his hopping around the room, trying not to trip over the legs as he pulls them up over his hips. I've missed that sight, even though our room at Kink Manor had a lot less space for hopping.

Once we're dressed, we hold hands and head toward the back door of the club where the rest of our crew seems to be waiting for something. Toby doesn't seem to notice everyone else's hesitation and pushes the door open, pulling me out right along with him.

"Yeah well maybe they should have just finished me off that night."

The anguish in Donnie's voice cuts through me, and it's like my brain decides it has had enough grief to last a lifetime.

"The fuck you just say?!" I shriek at him and I almost laugh as the white boys surrounding me go full on Casper at my outburst.

45

TOBY

I've never seen Shiloh this angry before. Hell, I don't think I've seen him more than slightly perturbed, but Donnie done fucked up tonight. Shy is seething next to me in the backseat of Donnie's car. I'm pretty sure it has nothing to do with what happened inside and everything to do with what we heard when I barged outside.

I feel kind of bad about that, interrupting his talk with Professor Barnes. I still feel weird about calling him by his first name, or rather his middle name... or a shortened version of it? I dunno. Until I graduate and know for a fact I won't have to take one of his classes again, I can't do it.

Donnie meets my eyes in the rearview mirror before making the turn to pull into the alley behind the coffee shop. He looks sad... and scared... and... Well, I'm not sure what else is there but it's sure as shit not happy.

"You guys need to talk," I say when he turns off the car. "I can get an Uber back to the house."

I open the door to get out, but Shy grabs my wrist and glares at me when I turn to him. Fuck. He's hot when he's all riled up like this.

"You aren't going anywhere except the both of you are going to march your lily white asses upstairs and we are *all* going to talk about this shit between us and get it all out in the open. I've got enough to be afraid of with Michael out there that I don't need to be afraid of losing anyone else. Got it?"

Holy Christ on a cracker... I think bossy Shiloh just made me pop a boner.

With a gulp, I nod and he releases my hand so that I can get out of the car. Leaving my pup gear in the trunk, I follow Donnie and Shiloh to a door marked PRIVATE and watch my kitten stomp up the stairs inside. I share a glance with the bigger man before he waves me ahead of him to go up the stairs. Even though I'm thoroughly turned on, right now, my heart is racing for other reasons.

Did Donnie just groan? Did he hurt himself?

"Do you have some sort of knee problems? I heard leg injuries are very common with college athletes and prevents a lot from going pro. Is that what happened to you? What did you play? You look really fit like you played something."

Stop babbling, ya ijit...

Donnie chuckles from behind me and I hear a crack followed by a flash of pressure on my ass. It takes a second for my body to realize he just whacked me on my ass.

"Did you just *spank* me?" I squeak out as I turn around, grasping the handrail desperately so that I don't embarrass myself further by falling down the stairs.

"You liked it," he leans down to whisper in my ear as he moves around me to enter his apartment, leaving the door open for me to follow.

Oh, fuck.

I did. I really fucking did.

46

DONNIE

The interlude with Toby on the stairs brings a smile to my face after the disastrous events of our night out. I never meant for the boys to see me at my worst. I sure as shit never wanted anyone to hear how I still feel about that night...especially Eric.

After my mouth fucked everything up by saying the quiet part out loud, Shiloh snatched my keys right off my belt loop and stormed off to the car, dragging a flabbergasted Toby along with him. I said a rushed goodbye to the rest of the guys, but Eric grabbed my wrist before I could run off.

"Do you really mean that? Do you really wish you had died that night?"

I probably looked like a fish with the way my mouth opened and closed repeatedly, but in the end, he didn't want my answer – not really.

"I sometimes do, too." His voice was pitched low

enough that it didn't carry to any of the others, and I looked at him. I *really* looked at him, probably for the first time. I finally saw that he truly doesn't blame me in any way. At the same time, he and I will always be marked and scarred by that night. He just got better at hiding the darkness. I just became a hermit.

The door closing behind me shakes me out of the memories from earlier. I look back at the entryway to see Toby toe-ing off his shoes and setting them next to Shiloh's. I noticed that habit of his immediately when he moved in, but I figured it was just something Shiloh was raised with, but now I'm not sure.

"You don't have to take your shoes off if you don't want to," I tell him as I head to the kitchen for a can of pop. "I usually don't bother unless I'm in for the night."

It would be a pain for me to have to constantly put them on and take them off during the days when I'm running up and down those stairs because I need something out of Walt's records for the shop.

Cracking open a Sprite, I lean back against the counter and watch Toby explore the space for a little bit. I'm guessing Shiloh went to his room for something – or to calm down. I've never seen him like that since he moved in, and judging by the looks on everyone else's faces, it's not common for him to get visibly angry.

The bit of happy that Toby managed to pull out of me vanishes as I remember the pain and anger on Shiloh's face when we were leaving the club. He wasn't supposed to hear me say that. No one was supposed to.

He watched his mama die. Matt's warning about the boy swims up in my mind.

"Scott is a bit OCD, so no shoes go past the entryway unless they've been thoroughly disinfected."

Toby's voice pulls me back again and I take another swig of my pop to try and remember what we were talking about. Shoes! That's it. I try to pull back from my worry about Shiloh to focus on the pup in front of me.

"I don't think I've met Scott yet. Is he a student like yinz?"

Toby giggles and flops down on the giant bean bag chair I put in the corner of the dining room for Shiloh's sun-napping. The thing instantly swallows him up. While he's struggling to escape from the thing, he answers my question.

"Scott is thirty-four, maybe thirty-five. I'm not sure the exact year, but he's almost old enough to be a father to me," he says with a smile. "Actually, where I grew up, that would be a definite possibility. The fact that all of my friends in high school graduated without popping out babies was kind of a miracle. Although, Alicia *was* six months pregnant when we walked for our diplomas."

Before I can get more amusing information out of the talkative pup, Shiloh emerges from his room in his pajama bottoms and a t-shirt that I recognize. He must have grabbed it from one of the boxes I tried to throw out. It's my old Tibalt University Hockey Program workout shirt. How the fuck did that thing survive the initial purge five years ago?

Toby jumps up and races to his best friend for a hug, but my entire body seizes up in fear and shame. There's no way this is a coincidence, right?

I lift my eyes to meet Shiloh's gaze over the top of Toby's blond head.

He knows.

47

SHILOH

I know it's here somewhere. I haven't let him throw out any boxes. It has to be here...

There it is!

I dig out the box of hockey stuff that is mostly just workout clothes and pull out the TU shirt. I know the history of the hockey team at Tibalt University. I mean, I lived in the same house with Eric for the last three years. I've witnessed the meltdowns, the self-hatred, the nightmares – all of it.

I figured it out the first time Eric went off his meds after I moved in. In my experience, people who were too friendly, too sweet, or too polite were the ones who would hurt me the most. People only showed their true colors when they knew you weren't going to squeal, when they had you trapped. I was hiding in the basement to get away from everyone when I heard Eli and Spencer fighting about it in the kitchen.

Everyone was talking about that night back when it

happened. A couple of the guys from my school were set to go to TU for sports scholarships, but had to scramble to find other schools who would take them and offer similar deals at the last minute. A *lot* of people were pissed off about the hockey program getting shut down. Most of those people blamed the wrong side for it, but you can't argue with stupid, not if you want to keep all the blood inside of your body in my experience.

When I put it together that the victim was one of my new roommates, that was when I started to trust the guys at Kink Manor. Then, when Toby showed up about a month later, I realized that some people are just genuinely good and nice and kind. He changed my view of the world so much without even knowing it.

But I never put it together about Donnie being a part of Eric's past until tonight. I knew they were friends through Matt, what with him being a professor with a caffeine addiction and all, but I never realized the connection with my favorite drag queen.

On the ride home, I was furious. After Mama... The only way I want to find out about anyone I know dying is from old age at this point. When I heard those words from Donnie, I wanted to lock him in a room where he couldn't follow through with it. I wanted to go back in time to destroy whoever put that in his head.

I can admit. I flew off the handle. I don't do it often. Mama always reminded me that I can't show my temper, not like the other kids. As I got older, I realized why. When confronted by anyone in authority, my skin color will never work in my favor... at least not in most situations. When I got hit, kicked, cut, and literally thrown down a flight of stairs in school, I got in trouble for saying a cuss word in the nurse's office.

Shaking my head to clear the unwelcome thoughts, I pull on the TU shirt, knowing it's time to push Donnie to open up to us. I'm not ready to lose either one of them, and it's about damn time the world gives me something good.

Coming out of my room, I barely make it two steps before my arms are filled with Toby. It's been a while since he's hugged me so tight, pressing his ear against my chest to listen to my heartbeat. I smile down at him, but he's not paying any attention.

Well in that case.

I look across the room to see my roommate, looking like he's going to be sick. I feel the smile fall off my face as he meets my eyes.

He's afraid.

"Let's grab a seat in the living room, pup," I say as I nudge Toby toward the couch. "We all need to have a nice little chat. It's time we put all of our pasts on the table so we can move into the future together."

Toby trips over his own feet and I have the option to let him fall on the couch by himself or bring us both down. I hold tight as we crash to the cushions and he lets out a squeak.

"Together? Like all *three* of us together? That kind of together?"

I push myself upright, leaving the stunned pup half sprawled on the seat next to me.

"If that's what you want," Donnie says with a hopeful look in my direction as he comes around the back of the sofa to sit in the recliner we picked up last weekend. I nod at him in response with a small smile.

Toby scrambles to sit up on the couch, almost kneeing himself in the eye in the process. I narrowly avoided a flying elbow myself.

"Oh, I want, Daddy. I want."

48

DONNIE

The sound of Toby calling me 'Daddy' does not give me any feelings but the icky kind.

"I am *so* not a Daddy. Pick another title, please." I grimace. Nothing against the Daddies of the world, but at best I am an Uncle as far as the dynamics go. I like littles and brats to hang out with, but I do not want one for myself. I don't want that kind of responsibility.

Shiloh mumbles something under his breath that I don't quite catch.

"Master won't work!" Toby tells him. "You're black! Or... at least close enough that some busybody tone-deaf do-gooder is going to go all crazy on him in the club if you're calling him Master."

"Ugh! What is with everyone's insistence that I can't use the terms I want just because my grandmother fucked a black man?!"

Shiloh falls back against the arm of the couch in exasperation and throws his legs over Toby's lap. "It's not like I'm going to give a shit what anyone there thinks outside of our friends and you know they won't care."

Resting my forearms on my thighs, I lean forward to be closer in case they start talking low again.

"You know he's right, Kitten," I say when it is obvious no one else is going to be talking. "There are a lot of people in the world right now who think everyone should think like them and they will make drama and confrontation where no one wants it just to feel better about themselves. I don't think it's a good idea to make it easy on them. There's another title for me. We just need to think about it."

He sighs and sits up, leaving his feet in Toby's lap.

"Fine," he grumbles. "But while we're thinking about it, you need to tell us what the fuck happened to you tonight. You were just gone and replaced with someone I haven't seen before..."

I gaze into his soulful copper eyes and sigh.

"As much as I'd rather talk about what happened with you in the bathroom, I suppose this is something you guys need to know about me."

Taking a deep breath, I tell them my story.

"Almost six years ago, I was a junior at Tibalt University and was the left winger on the second line for the hockey team. It had been a season where everything aligned perfectly. Our guys led the division in goals, assists, points, save percentage – you name it. It was fucking magical. I was even approached by a few scouts telling me I should put my name in for the NHL draft that year."

"You must have been really good," Toby says with awe in his voice. "Like Gretzky good, right?"

A surprised laugh barks out of my chest at his question.

"Pup, the only player who I would ever place in the same stratosphere as The Great One would be Le Magnifique."

At the confused glances pointed my way, I elaborate.

"Wayne Gretzky holds most of the scoring records in the NHL from his career and he was given the nickname of The Great One. Now, there's a lot of arguments about how much of a difference it made with him having the teams he did around him, but the numbers still put him at the top objectively."

"What about Le Magician?" Toby asks with an inquisitive tilt of his head.

"Le Magnifique is one of the nicknames given to Mario Lemieux of the Pittsburgh Penguins," I tell him and I see the recognition in his eyes. "He was also nick-named Super Mario but that's besides the point. Most of Pittsburgh will tell you that had Lemieux been healthy his whole career, he would have easily surpassed Gret-zky, despite having less support from management and a less skilled team surrounding him."

"I thought it was cuz he had cancer or something?" Shiloh asks before Toby could jump in again and mangle more of hockey history. He really needs to learn this stuff if he plans on sticking around Pittsburgh after gradua-tion. If there's one thing Pittsburgh knows, it's their sports history. Well, that and putting fries on everything.

"Hodgkins Lymphoma, yeah," I tell Shiloh. "He also had horrible back issues so he retired early to fight the cancer and heal up. Then he came back and damn near broke the league with how on fire he was. He didn't retire for good until he was in his forties, even after buying the team to keep hockey in Pittsburgh. But that time off really messes with people's heads in this city. Around here, sixty-six will always be better than ninety-nine."

"Wha..."

"Their jersey numbers," Shiloh slams his palm over Toby's mouth and interrupts his next question. "Back to your story, please."

"So to answer your earlier question, Toby, no – I was not nor ever could possibly be Gretzky good. Professional hockey was never my goal. It was only ever a way to pay for school for me."

Before Toby could interrupt again, I delve into the details.

At the end of the regular season every year, the team would throw a huge bash at the house of one of our former players. Streaker wasn't good enough to go pro, but he managed to make a decent living as an investment banker or something like that. He was one of those guys that peaked in college and wanted to re-live his glory days through us, so he bought a house specifically to use for parties.

The house was located in an area where the local cops didn't have jurisdiction, so it had to be the county who would respond if anyone ever called it in. It was perfect because they kept an old police scanner in the kitchen tuned into the county sheriff's frequency so we would be able to ditch or hide the booze if it was called in.

"After winning our last home game, we were riding high off our record breaking season. We were setting up the house for the party when this random chick came up and started talking to Rafe, our captain. I heard the details of the discussion since I was close by, but most of the rest of the guys were off in other parts of the house. She offered him five grand to drug some rich boy and toss him in a bedroom for the night."

"Vad wad bishy Babrina?"

Shiloh laughs and wipes his hand against Toby's shirt when he pulls it away from his best friend's mouth. "I guess that won't work going forward."

Rolling my eyes, I level the pup with a smirk.

"Yes, it was Sabrina Carlisle," I tell him. "Rafe took the money and announced to the boys that we had money for more booze and sent me and a couple of the younger guys out to get more for the party. By the time we got back, almost everything was set up and I didn't think anything of it until shit went wrong."

Taking a breath to center myself, I lean back and stare at the ceiling. If I'm going to get through this, I can't be looking at them. This is where they find out how horribly I failed their friend.

This is where I lose them.

49

TOBY

Donnie looks like he's expecting a two ton anvil to fall through the ceiling and crush him – and he'd welcome it. I look over at Shiloh and the sad smile on his face tells me he already knows where this story is going. I mean, with Lucky's bitch of an ex-wife involved, I already know it's not going anywhere good, even if I hadn't heard what Donnie said back at the club.

"I saw when Rafe put the drugs into Eric's root beer."

ERIC? The guy they decided to drug was Eric? OUR Eric?

"I stood by and did nothing as he and another senior practically dragged him upstairs. Easy money, right? I waited for them to come down. After five minutes, I went up to see what the fuck was taking so long to put him in a room and leave. I opened the door and saw..."

I don't want to hear this. Eric is one of my best friends. He's family. Hell, he brought me back a slice of my own family with Uncle Robert. I know the gist of what happened to him. I don't want the details, not unless he tells me himself. In my head, I am trying to think of anything I can to distract myself from hearing this.

Did I run out of toaster pastries at the house? Did Jay steal my Lunchables?

"... the next thing I knew I was in the hallway outside of the door. I could still hear the sounds..."

The disgust on Donnie's face is plain to see. I missed a lot of the story, but I know enough about what happened to Eric to know that this man in front of me would have never condoned it.

"I remember Rafe spitting on me before he walked down the stairs, leaving me alone on the third floor. Everything is blank from there until I woke up in the hospital the next day. My leg was fractured in two places, my left ankle shattered. My collarbone snapped. My right ulna had broken through my arm, tearing the muscles and ligaments. And I had four broken ribs that the doctors say I was lucky didn't puncture anything."

Now, I know I'm not the smartest pup out there, but what in the actual fuck? How much did I miss? Maybe he'll recap it for me. I just don't understand why his teammates would have hurt him that much. Didn't they need him to win more games? Doesn't that usually keep guys on sports teams safe?

"... tried to get me to rescind my statement to the police. Even some fancy lawyers that I now know were sent by Eric's father tried to get me to say I didn't see who or what I thought I did, that my teammates didn't almost kill me because I told them it was wrong to rape someone."

Why are all the rich people douche canoes? I mean, not Eric or Lucky or Gramps... but like these fucktwats.

"Before that night, hockey was my life. Those men were my brothers. After waking up in that hospital and having the world turn against me, I grew to hate it all. The injuries I got that night killed any shot I had of ever playing competitively again, but the reaction of the school and the community made me never want to lace up skates at all.

"Even my own parents told me to just keep my mouth shut and find a minor league team to play for. Their exact words were: '*We didn't shell out all that money for you to throw it all away for some fairy boy who was too stupid to watch his drink*'... That was the last thing my father said to me."

I can't fucking take it any more. I launch myself off the couch and onto Donnie's lap, nearly overturning the recliner in the process.

Fuck his parents.

Fuck his school.

Fuck his teammates.

Fuck that fucking brotherhood bullshit mentality.

"You did the right thing. Fuck them. I'm proud of you," I tell him as I grip him in the tightest hug I can possibly give a man who is taller and wider and infinitely stronger than me. What can I say? The man is built. He is a tree I definitely want to climb.

50

SHILOH

Seeing Toby embrace Donnie makes me all warm and fuzzy on the inside. Now that I know his side of the story, beyond what was put into the papers, I have a better understanding of what he's feeling. He's got survivor's guilt, just like me. Only difference is Eric is still alive.

Donnie doesn't see that his teammates were shit people. He doesn't see that his captain pushed the people who would have objected onto that booze run so that he could organize it with the ones he knew would help him with his twisted fucked up plan.

His captain sounds like he'd get along with Michael. Thinking of my stepbrother sends a shiver through me that doesn't go unnoticed.

"What was that for, Kitten?" Donnie asks me as he adjusts Toby into a more comfortable position on his lap. No one likes a bouncy pup's knee too close to their family jewels.

I bring my legs up to my chest and exhale loudly.

"I just thought about the fact that your captain and my stepbrother probably would have gotten along swimmingly. Two peas in a sadistic, fucked up, abusive pod."

Toby looks like he wants to come cuddle me, but Donnie still needs him right now. Plus, the two of them can hold each other back. Leave it to me to fall in love with two guys with anger issues and a protective streak fifty miles wide...

I don't want to talk about my past right now. Judging by the sky outside, it's late enough to justify going to bed, and I really want to go to bed with both of them.

"You haven't seen him again, have you?" Toby asks with a growl.

Shaking my head, I get up to grab myself a drink from the kitchen. Donnie loves his Sprite, but I prefer water. He finally talked me into getting the flavored seltzer waters, but it's still better than pop.

"I have the restraining order and don't go anywhere off campus unless it's with one of the guys. If he tries to come after me, it would mean he's gotten dumber from being behind bars."

Donnie lifts Toby off his lap and comes over to wrap me in a hug. I like the fact that he doesn't hold back or hesitate like the guys from the house do. They never quite understood that my touch aversion has more to deal with me being surprised than with me not wanting to be touched at all. Both of my men give me ample time and space to step away if I want to.

Resting my cheek on Donnie's shoulder, I look over at

Toby. He's just standing in the living room, watching us with a sad look on his face.

Fuck that.

I reach out my hand for him to come to us. I'm not going to exclude either of them. Tonight made me realize I want them both. For once in my life, I'm going to take what I want.

"I think we need to bring our pup into this, Owner," I mutter as I turn my face to Donnie's neck. Placing soft kisses up from his collarbone to just behind his ear, I finish with a whisper. "Toby has always wanted to visit the Eiffel Tower."

Donnie's head falls back as he groans in obvious pleasure. I'm not sure if he's reacting to what I've said or to the fact that I can't seem to stop licking and kissing his neck. Either way, I can't help but notice his body has certainly taken an interest in things. I wasn't sure if I could be a bottom before tonight, but between the plug at the club and now, I might be willing to try it for Donnie.

"Where do you want me?"

Toby's breathless voice comes from right next to us, making Donnie startle before stepping back in laughter. It takes an effort, but I pull my attention away to look at our pup. Not even two seconds later, we're gasping for air while Toby looks confused by us acting like a couple of hyenas.

51

DONNIE

Wiping the tears from the corner of my eyes, I pull Toby into a hug. The pup must have heard Shiloh's whisper to me because he threw his clothing off and raced over to us. He was just standing there, in the middle of our dining area, in full view of the open window, wearing only what God gave him.

"Sweet pup. Never change," Shiloh gasps out as I tilt Toby's mouth up for a kiss.

While I'm experiencing the exuberant make out styles of Tobias Grady, Shiloh goes to the window to pull the curtains closed. Pulling back from the kiss, I notice Toby is still moving his lips for a few seconds, making me chuckle. The kid has enthusiasm for sure.

Shiloh slinks up to us, reminding me so much of his kitten self than the man I've been sharing a home with these past weeks. Giving me a wink, he pulls Toby's mouth to his own while keeping eye contact with me.

Oh, fuck this is probably the hottest thing I've ever seen, let alone experienced.

"We can do this here or my room," I say while I watch Shiloh devour the man in my arms. "My room has lube and toys and a few other things you might be interested in."

"Toys?!" Toby pulls away from Shiloh's mouth to look at me excitedly. "Oh, I love toys! Do you have a cock cage? I've always wanted one, but I don't have the money to spend on anything but school since I bought the pup gear."

Shiloh puts his hand on Toby's throat from behind and squeezes lightly. The pup and I both let out a groan. I can feel my dick start to leak from the sight of my kitten's dark hand against the milky skin of our pup's throat. How perfect would it be if one of these boys was into breath play?

I stop hugging Toby and pull him by the wrist into my bedroom. I notice Shiloh keeps his hand at our pup's throat for the walk down the short hallway. As much as I don't want to leave them to play by themselves without me seeing it, I turn to my closet to start gathering some items for us for tonight.

The lube is next to the bed, but I want to see how my boys do with some restraints. I have no intention of this being a one shot kind of night.

"On the bed, pup," I order as I grab the lube and add it to the pile of items on the bed. "You, too, Kitten."

Toby leaps onto my California King bed without hesitation, but Shiloh quirks a brow before sauntering over and climbing to the center. One is looking at the pile like it's Christmas morning while the other looks skeptical.

"A straight jacket?" Shiloh picks up the leather piece I had custom made for a sub I had played with a few years ago. He was about Toby's size and ended up moving away after he graduated college. It was meant to be his graduation gift, but he ghosted me.

"Not for you," I say as I quickly put Toby's arms into the sleeves while he is distracted by the rest of the pile. Zipping up the back, I yank the hair on top of Toby's head so that I can give him another kiss to distract him further. The flash of pain is followed by a look of utter bliss before I reclaim his mouth.

Shiloh must have understood what I was intending because he wraps Toby's arms around to secure the straps of the jacket. I don't release our pup from the kiss until I notice Shiloh has sat back on his heels. Looking down, I see that he managed to not only secure Toby's arms, but also the straps that go between the legs to hold the jacket in place.

It takes a few seconds for Toby's brain to readjust and notice he's been restrained. Watching him start squirming and flopping on the bed is as humourous as it is arousing.

"Are you ok with this, Toby?" I ask him honestly. "Stoplight colors will do for tonight."

"So fucking GREEN!" he growls out as he arches up on the bed, still struggling against the bonds. "I want more!"

Shiloh picks up a muzzle gag from the pile of items I placed on the bed and looks at me questioningly. "Can I put this on him?"

Toby is nodding enthusiastically, but I freeze. "I won't take away his ability to safeword."

Both of them look at me in surprise. I don't know if I can do this. I can't have him in the straightjacket and a gag. It's not safe at all.

Shiloh takes my hand and places it on his cheek, forcing me to look at him.

"Toby loves being gagged and restrained. His nonverbal safeword for his hands is 3 snaps, but if his hands are sealed like this, he will click his heels 3 times."

"Like Dorothy," Toby pipes up helpfully. "I really do like this a lot, but if you need to be a bit more vanilla in the beginning, I understand. I can be a handful and mrph..."

Shiloh shoves the ball-gag part of the muzzle into Toby's open mouth while he is still talking and secures the straps to lock the harness in place. I notice he grabbed the one where the muzzle part is removeable. Before I can ask why, he rolls Toby onto his stomach and pulls a piece of rope through the top of the harness to attach to Toby's arms, effectively forcing our pup to keep his head back.

"If you want to use a spreader or secure his legs in some way, three grunts also work for his safeword when he's trussed up."

Toby makes a sequence of grunts in groups of threes to prove the point, and I'm wondering how the fuck I stumbled upon my wet dream like this. Not only do these boys understand bondage and restraints, they also have a predetermined system of safety protocols for play.

"Oh, Pet, I am going to have so much fun with you," I murmur as I stand up to take off my clothes. Once I'm completely naked, I go into the closet to grab my spreader bar. I guess we are going all out tonight.

52

TOBY

All I can see is Shy's glorious dick in front of me as he kneels with his legs open on the bed. I can hear Donnie getting undressed, but with how Shy tied off the head harness, I can't turn around to look without full on pinwheeling on the mattress. And I know that Shiloh will pin me if I attempt it.

Ooooh, it's tempting.

But I'm enjoying the sight of my kitten's cock perking up in response to the vision that he's seeing. Donnie was an athlete so his body is probably fucking god-like. I mean, it looks that way with clothes on, so I can't wait to get a glimpse with clothes off.

There's a flash of something in the corner of my eye and it sounds like there's noise coming from the closet. What else could he be pulling out?

"You're getting everything you want, pup," Shiloh whispers as he runs the back of his fingers along my cheek. "It was never safe enough to go this far with just us two and definitely not at the club. We can trust Donnie. I want him to own us both."

"Mmmmmmm!" I try to make a sound of agreement since I can't nod.

"I knew you'd agree," he says, leaning down to plant a kiss on my forehead.

The feel of leather against my ankle has me kick out involuntarily, but Donnie just chuckles from behind me. I feel his weight drop onto my back as he sits astride me. Rolling my eyes up, I see him and Shiloh kiss above me as I struggle to take a breath.

Pressing is something I've always been curious about. Hell, most of the breath play scenarios are interesting to me. But it's extremely dangerous to do it without an experienced partner.

I feel a hand against my neck, and before the black spots really start to encroach on my vision, the weight is lifted off. I suck in deep breaths through my nose and float on the verge of subspace for a bit. I'm not sure how long I drifted, but when I come back to myself, I see Donnie's hand stroking Shy's cock less than six inches from my face.

"Come for me, Kitten," Donnie's voice seems to vibrate through me even though he's not talking to me. I try to bring my legs together to get some friction on my aching dick, but realize I can't. I can lift my feet off the bed and even push up slightly on my knees if I wiggle. But my legs are fixed apart.

He put me in a spreader. Oh, my stars! I should buy a lottery ticket. I've never been so lucky.

Before I can even fully process this, Shiloh cries out above me. Ropes of cum shoot out of his cock and land on my face while I struggle to move. I'm not sure if I want to be closer or farther away, but I know my body wants to move, wants release.

"Ah, ah, ah," Donnie scolds as his hand slaps down on my bare ass cheek. "Good pups know how to Stay. Clean him up, Kitten."

Closing my eyes, I wait for the tissues or cloth to rub against my face to clean me up. Instead, my eyes fly open when I realize Shiloh is *licking* me clean. My hips start rutting against the mattress of their own volition.

This is too freaking sexy.

This is my fifteen year old porn-loving mind's wet dream.

SMACK!

Donnie's hand makes contact with the other cheek and I can't stop the pitiful whine that escapes my throat.

"Looks like we need to do some training with our pup," he says as I feel his weight leaving the bed. Shiloh gets up as well. Before I can safeword to let them know that leaving me alone is a hard limit for me, I am being dragged across the bed by the spreader bar.

When my waist reaches the edge of the bed, the bar is dropped so my feet are on the floor. Hands pull me to a standing position. Before I can get my bearings, what with being stuck staring at the ceiling and all, Donnie hoists me up, using his shoulder, and carries me a short distance. I don't understand why except that I'm completely in the open and won't have the bed to fall onto if I try to move.

"Now, Toby, I'm sure our kitten wants some more cream. Would you help him with that while I have my own treat?"

"Hhrm?"

My question is answered by a dark chuckle as wet heat engulfs my cock. I jump and would have fallen, except for the strong arms that wrap around me from behind. Donnie looks down into my startled eyes with a smirk.

"Time for my own treat," he whispers in my ear as he disappears again from my sight.

53

SHILOH

Toby and I have given each other hand jobs before, but never crossed that line before today. It's not that I never wanted to. I was always afraid that I would lose him if we ever went that far. Somehow, with the addition of Donald Hastings, things just click in a way that I can't describe.

I roll my eyes up to watch as Donnie glides his hands down Toby's restrained body. Watching him kneel behind our pup while I'm in front is a bit of a power trip. Toby might be the one standing, but he's completely in our control.

Donnie's hand caresses my right cheek before sliding down to my throat and giving it a small squeeze.

Our control? I meant Owner's control.

Holy fuck this is hot. I just came and my dick is already trying to rally.

I pull off Toby's dick to start licking it like a popsicle and flicking the tip with my tongue. I may not be attracted to women, but I heard enough techniques from the girls in school to know how to work my tongue effectively. The alphabet thing is a crapshoot for dicks, and apparently for clits according to Avery. Rolling the 'R' like you need to do for other languages tends to make for the best skillset, according to most I've talked to.

Glancing around Toby's hip, Donnie winks at me and I have an idea what's coming. I suck the tip of Toby's cock between my lips and wait for it. Two seconds later, his hips ram forward, pushing his dick toward the back of my throat. It's a good thing I was prepared because vomiting on my best friend's crotch while we're prepping him for an Eiffel Tower is not sexy.

Would this be a reverse Eiffel Tower? Inverted?

The squeal coming from Toby's throat combined with the jerking of his hips reminds me that I have a job to do here and terminology can stay a mystery until I can Google it.

Relaxing my throat further, I let Toby continue to thrust down my throat while Donnie prepares his ass. We are trying to fulfill a fantasy for our pup, after all.

"I think he's stretched enough. Ready to take his cream, Kitten?"

I let go of Toby's balls and reach through his legs to give Donnie a thumbs up. The only response and warning I receive is a snort before our pup squeals an even higher pitch and starts to buck his hips in earnest. I do my best to move with him, but when he tenses up, I almost pull off. The first spurt of his release hits the back of my throat and I have to fight not to gag as it hits that one spot on my soft palate. Fighting against my initial reaction, I start to swallow.

The discomfort is soon forgotten as the bliss practically radiates off our swaying pup and I sit back on my heels to look up at my best friend, all trussed up and flying high on the endorphins.

"We're not done yet," Donnie says as he grabs Toby by the waist and positions him on his knees back on the bed and holds up a condom. "Do you want front or back, Kitten?"

54

TOBY

It could have been hours. It could have been days. I don't fucking care. Waking up smooshed between my two favorite people after a marathon of kinky fuckery is how I want to live the rest of my life. From the moment Shy's dick exploded onto my face and he licked it clean, I swear my brain shut off. I want to remember details, but everything just blurs together in a kaleidoscope of kinktopia.

After they made me the center in the reverse version, they proceeded to make my fifteen year old self's fantasy come true and made me the center in their Eiffel Tower. I think I blacked out from sheer sexual overload when Shiloh was pounding in my ass while I was choking on Donnie's schlong and the two of them were making out above me. I have a vague recollection of being released from everything and held upright in a shower, but it's all fuzzy.

"Toby, go back to sleep," Shiloh mumbles before rolling over to give me his back. Usually at home, we swap spoon positions like this when we wake each other up, but I'm not tired anymore. I glance to my other side and see Donnie sprawled on his back with his right arm above his head. Pretty sure he had that arm around my waist when we settled in after the shower.

Shower. Bathroom. Need to pee...

I wiggle my way carefully down the center of the bed, grateful that Donnie is not the kind of person who tucks in the bottom of the blankets, and race to the bathroom to empty my bladder. As I am washing my hands, I look at myself in the mirror. I can't stop the goofy grin that shows up on my face when I notice the faint red marks from where the straps of the harness and straightjacket dug into my skin during my struggles.

Glancing down, I'm really glad that my morning wood waited until after I peed to pop up. It's not easy to aim when you're hard.

After flushing and washing my hands for the *second* time this morning, I glance at the clock on the wall in the hallway and see that it is fuck early o'clock.

I should go back to bed. I want to go back to cuddling with my... what do I call them?

My boyfriends? I think it's too early for that one.

My lovers? Ugh – too soap opera-y

My best friend and my... What did Shy call him to get him all riled up last night?

OWNER

Oh my sweet baby Jesus, that's perfect!

Peeking into the bedroom, I see that my best friend and our Owner are still asleep. If I go back in there now, they will just wake up and then all of us will be awake at a quarter till bird thirty. Instead, I think it's time to reveal to Shy where I've been going during the evenings. It's time for me to show off what I've learned, especially since I'll be graduating from there in a couple weeks.

It's time to prove I'm not a screw up.

I'm gonna make them the best damn breakfast on the planet as a thank you for last night.

I skip over to the pantry and realize that breakfast might be reaching. Pulling open the fridge, I notice the trend continues and the smile falls off my face.

Where the fuck is the food?

55

DONNIE

Most days, I have my alarm set for five so that I can get up, start the coffee down in the shop, get a run in, and shower before opening up at six thirty. So why is my phone going off at four forty three?

I stumble out of bed to the living room to get my damn phone from wherever I dropped it last night. Digging iy out of my jacket pocket, I notice there is only five percent battery left.

I want to strangle whoever is blowing up my phone at this hour. Considering it's close enough to the time when I need to be awake, I head to the kitchen to plug in my phone there while I get some caffeine in me to wake up.

Shiloh insisted we needed to get a Keurig, and I'm grateful to it as my zombified ass stumbles through the apartment in the dark. I'm not going to lie. It's fucking convenient to have a single cup brewed in under a minute. But for taste, I still prefer what I brew downstairs compared to any prepackaged stuff, no matter how convenient this might be.

As I take the first sip, my phone starts to vibrate across the counter. Glancing at the screen, I see it's the notification for the doorbell camera in the alley. The damn app must have updated and reset the sensitivity settings. I swear every time it happens, I'll get alerts for every car that uses the alley, every stray cat that wanders by.

By the third notification in under five minutes, I pick up the phone and decide to check the app. Not enough magic bean juice is in my system yet for figuring out the settings to get it to stop. I take another sip of my coffee while I wait for the app to connect and almost choke when I see Toby on the screen with his arms wrapped around himself, bouncing from side to side.

I hit the button for the microphone and run back to my room to grab pants to throw on.

"Boy, what the fuck are you doing outside?!" I growl out as I yank on the first pair of pants I see, only to realize these are Shiloh's and way too tight. Fuck it. They'll do.

"I wanted to surp-p-prise you with b-b-breakfast," he manages to get out and holds up a bag to the camera. *Fuck!* Ignoring my shoes, I rip open the apartment door and fly down the stairs to the back door. Throwing it open, I see him shivering in his t-shirt and jeans with about a dozen grocery bags at his feet.

"Get your ass inside! It's barely forty degrees out here."

It's way too cold out to be outside without a coat. I

know I'm only wearing pants, but there's frost showing on the edge of the dumpster. We're in that weird part of autumn in Southwestern Pennsylvania where it's seventy something one day and then it barely reaches fifty the next day. Anyone who has lived here for more than a year should know better than to brave an October morning without layering up.

What the hell was he thinking? It's too fucking cold out to not be wearing a coat for anything longer than a dumpster run, and it's obvious he went a hell of a lot farther than the dumpster. Glancing at the logo on the bags, I realize he didn't go to a local store either. I don't even know this place or where it is, and I've lived here my whole damn life. I reach down to grab the bags and nudge Toby into the warmth of the building.

Locking the door behind me, I try to calm my breathing. I know I shouldn't have yelled, but seeing him on the screen shivering scared the shit out of me. I didn't even notice that he wasn't in the apartment...

"How long were you waiting out there?" I ask pulling him into my arms in the darkness of the stairwell, rubbing my hands along his bare arms to warm him up. "And why the fuck did you go shopping? Nothing in this area opens before six, not since the pandemic."

Toby sniffles a bit and huddles in on himself before replying, "I've been up for about two hours, maybe three. I wanted to surprise you with breakfast, but y'all are worse than Eric when it comes to keeping real food stocked."

I chuckle at his response. Having gotten to know Eric

over the last six months or so, I have to agree. He and Matt really don't do well at keeping food in the house. Ms. Sara, Matt's mother, really spoils them with premade meals.

"And the store? Where the hell did you find somewhere open at this hour?"

He pulls back from my embrace, but tucks in on himself like he wants to disappear. He's still shivering. He obviously needs the comfort and warmth, but he's denying himself for some reason.

Note to self: I need to be careful using admonishments for the pup.

"I'm not mad at you, Toby," I tell him and pull him back into my arms. My fingers under his chin lift his gaze up to meet mine. "You just scared the shit out of me before I had enough coffee in my system. Now, where did you go shopping?"

He shakes his head out of my grip and snuggles in closer to my chest. His mumbled response is complete gobble-de-gook as far as my under-caffeinated brain can comprehend. Rubbing his back, I ask him to repeat himself a bit louder.

"There's a Korean grocer about a mile away from here," he says with a sigh and backs away to start grabbing up the bags. "The son was in a few classes with me last year and he lets me come in and shop whenever he's there, even if they aren't technically open. He stays up late to talk to his extended family in Seoul, so I'm not putting him out or anything.

"Plus, this way I'm ahead on my step count for the day, right?"

Taking a deep breath, I try not to overreact. Not only did this precious boy go grocery shopping at three in the fucking morning, he walked a mile each way without wearing a coat or having any way of getting back inside.

"Did you even..."

Before I can ask about his phone, because lord knows I have noticed that he didn't once try to call or text, a blood curdling scream echoes down the stairwell from my home. Glass shatters as Toby drops the bags in his hands and races up the stairs. I'm barely half a second behind him.

56

TOBY

Don is going to be pissed at me. I don't want to wake him up before the ass crack of dawn. Hell, there's another hour or so before you can even start to consider it bird thirty, but I can't take standing outside in the cold for much longer. I would try to call Shiloh, but my phone is in my hoodie pocket — the hoodie still laying on the bean bag chair inside the apartment.

I'm a fucking idiot for forgetting my hoodie.

Not only am I freezing, but I also have no way of calling for a rideshare to take me home – not that I necessarily want to go home. I want to spend more time with Donnie and Shy, but in my rush to surprise them with breakfast, I forgot that I wouldn't be able to get back in.

I've never had to deal with having a locked door between me and my home before. Growing up in a small Alabama town, we didn't lock our door because the only time the house was empty was when we were all out as a family, and my parents took care of locking and unlocking the house. Kink Manor is never locked. We all have locks on our individual rooms, but the house itself is never locked.

Wait a second...

Did I just refer to Shy's apartment as home?

Of course it's home. Home is wherever Shiloh is.

Before I manage to get my mind wrapped around my brain's epiphany, the backdoor flies open and I'm face to face with an irate coffee shop owner. He practically throws me inside and gathers up all the bags I had set down while I paced to keep warm.

While he yells at me, I struggle to keep myself present. I never could handle being yelled at. It reminds me of my grandfather and how worthless he makes everyone feel. It reminds me of how I've only ever been a disappointment. *Maybe I should just grab my hoodie and go...*

My eyes lock onto Don's and I find myself relaxing in his arms. I know he's not happy, but he says he was worried for me. Has anyone ever worried about me other than Shy? I mean, my father and Uncle Robert seem to, but one summer doesn't really make up for twenty years of feeling like I'm a permanent disappointment.

Don starts to ask me something, but Shiloh's scream echoes off the walls of the stairwell. I don't stop to think. I race up the stairs. I don't give a fuck if the door's closed or not, I will break through steel to get to my kitten when he needs me.

Luckily for Don's wallet, the door to the apartment is

open, and I rush back to the bedroom where I last saw Shiloh. I am used to dealing with carpeting and *not* wearing shoes, so when I tumble into the doorframe, I'm somewhat surprised.

I ignore the pain in my shoulder and push back to my feet to stumble to the bed where Shiloh is thrashing violently. He's gone beyond nightmare into full on night terror mode.

"Don't touch him!" I say just loud enough for Don to hear above Shy's whimpers when he reaches for our kitten. "He won't wake up until it's done and he'll only feel worse if he hurts you."

He looks as anguished as I know I feel, but he gives me a nod before grabbing some clothes and heading out in the hall to the bathroom. The second I hear the lock click on the door, I stuff my fist into my mouth to hold back my sobs as I watch the man I love more than life itself suffer through the hell of his past.

57

SHILOH

The smell of bacon is the first thing I notice waking up. That is the one thing I really enjoy about this apartment over living in Kink Manor. Don is very quiet in the mornings to the point where I don't usually hear him until he comes back after his morning run. Usually, I wake up to the smell of the coffee from downstairs, but bacon is a welcome change.

Do we even have bacon?

I sit up and my confusion intensifies as I notice that I am not in *my* room. The sheets that are tangled around my naked body are not mine... *NAKED?*

A quick glance around the room and the only piece of my clothing I can see is my t-shirt. *Where the fuck are my pants?*

I don't see my pants, but I do see the straight jacket and spreader bar over by the closet and the memories of last night start to flow back into my head. The sounds we coaxed out of Toby before we all collapsed in exhaustion have my dick taking notice first thing in the morning.

Now, if only I had some pants to cover up, I could go out and see what the fuck is going on and discover where the fuck the bacon came from.

Ultimately, I grab a pair of sweats from Don's drawer and yank my t-shirt from last night over my head. This will have to do for now. After a quick trip to the bathroom to relieve myself and brush my teeth, I plan to find out what my best friend and my roommate are up to at this ungodly hour of the morning. But first I really need to get this morning wood to disappear.

"How often do they happen?" Don's voice carries down the hallway as my dick finally gets the memo from my bladder. Toby always gets a kick out of the fact that I sit for my morning bathroom routine, but I refuse to make a mess trying to aim a hard dick to piss with a boner. Having dealt with my stepbrother and his nasty ass friends made me hyper-vigilant about making messes.

Toby's response is too soft for me to make out over the sounds in the bathroom. He doesn't sound like my carefree pup. I rush through washing up and try to keep calm. Did we hurt him last night?

"I can usually calm him down before they get as bad as that was."

I skid to a halt to see Don and Toby standing shoulder to shoulder in the kitchen. Toby is facing the stove, but Don is leaning against the counter next to him, looking at whatever is on the stovetop.

"I didn't know," Don says before he glances my way and startles. "Good morning, Kitten. Did we wake you up?"

Toby spins around and almost smacks Don in the face with the spatula in his hand.

"You're awake!" he says with a smile that's a bit too bright. "Morning!"

My brain is still struggling to come online, but it finally registers to me what is wrong with this picture. "Since when do you cook?"

Toby looks a bit like a kicked puppy, and I hate myself for putting that look on his face. I hurry over and pull him into my arms while Don reaches over to turn off the burner. I see that there's French toast, scrambled eggs, and bacon already piled up on counter. It looks like the potatoes still in the pan are the last bit of breakfast to be done.

"I didn't mean it like that, Tobes. I've just never seen you show any interest in cooking. You've never tried to cook at the manor. Even Lucky shows more interest in cooking than you do."

He pulls back from me and swipes at his cheeks, making me feel like even more of an ass for my careless remark. Toby only cries watching movies.

Don hands me my mug, the coffee made just the way I like it. I didn't even notice him making it.

"It was supposed to be a surprise," our pup says turning back to the stove and turning the burner back on. "I was going to invite you to my graduation and then cook a feast for everyone, but then I got into my head that I should make you guys breakfast to thank you for last night."

I sip at my coffee and look at my roommate. He looks just as confused as I do. There is not enough coffee in the world to keep up with Toby's brain sometimes.

"First things first," I set my mug down to be able to wrap my arms around Toby from behind. "I'm not sure about how Donnie feels, but last night is definitely something that you don't need to thank me for. It was absolutely my pleasure."

"Seconded," Don murmurs from the side and I watch as he presses a kiss to Toby's temple. "It's been a very long time since I've had someone trust me enough to let loose like that. I loved making you soar."

I chuckle at the shiver that runs through our pup as he turns off the stove again. This time, it's because the food is done unfortunately. I let go and step back so he can plate the potatoes, and we all pile up our individual plates and head to the living room to eat.

"As for the rest of your statement," Toby looks up at me from his spot on the floor in between the couch and the coffee table. "What do you mean about graduation? We don't finish until for another year."

Toby swallows the food in his mouth and gives us both a sheepish grin.

"So y'all know how I work at night?"

I nod because it was something that he always fought with Eli about. The Kink Manor resident sadist likes to keep tabs on everyone, and it always bothered the hell out of him that Toby refused to tell anyone where he worked – especially since Toby paid his rent in advance for the whole year and as far as all of us saw, he didn't have any other expenses to need a job.

"I actually don't have a job." The words tumble out of his mouth before he stuffs his face full of French toast. Don raises an eyebrow in question, but I'm floored. It actually hurts a bit that my best friend has been lying to be for the last three years.

"So, what have you been doing three nights a week for the last three years?" I try to keep the pain out of my voice, but his flinch tells me I didn't succeed.

He sets down his fork and turns to me. "I enrolled in culinary school practically the second I touched down in Pittsburgh. I had to cancel my housing at W.U. to afford it, but Jay had already brought me home as a stray at that point.

"He was my driver from the airport. We got stuck in traffic on the parkway heading into the tunnels, and he convinced me to meet everyone after I told him how I came here instead of the conversion camp my mother wanted me to go to... I just never really left Kink Manor after that."

58

DONNIE

Watching Toby cook in my kitchen unlocked something inside of me. I want to see this every single morning. What would it be like to go for my run and come back to a full breakfast cooked by my pup while I rouse my sleepy kitten before the sun comes up every day? That would be paradise...

The kitten in question interrupts our conversation, and we sit down to eat after a tense couple of minutes when my roommate questions his best friend's cooking. I don't see any issue, but based on the conversation they are having, it appears that Toby has been hiding the fact that he's been taking culinary classes for years.

This seems to be something that they need to get through. Lies have a way of tearing people apart, even when they are well-intentioned.

"...I came here instead of the conversion camp my mother wanted me to go to..."

Hash browns are not supposed to go down the wind

pipe, but holy fuck! Did he seriously just casually mention that his mother tried to send him to a conversion camp?!

Toby gets up and pats me on the back while I feel like I'm hacking up my left lung. Judging by the nonchalant way he spoke about it, I could almost believe that it doesn't bother him that the woman who gave birth to him wanted to send him to hell on earth. But his eyes are eerily empty for him. I'll let him hold onto his pain for now.

As I finally stop coughing enough to choke down some coffee, he sits back on the floor in front of his plate. "I kept it secret because I didn't want to risk seeing you guys disappointed if I fucked up and failed. By the time I realized making food wasn't only a hyper-fixation for my ADHD, I didn't know how to tell you guys. With Scott always handling the food and then the stuff with Lucky showing up, it got harder and harder to find a way to say something."

Shiloh slides off the couch to join Toby on the floor and pulls him into his side. I can see the pain they are trying to hide from each other. It's obvious to anyone with half a brain that these two love each other deeply and are willing to do just about anything to make sure that they aren't a burden to the other. They need someone to step in and show them that it's alright to feel what they feel and rely on each other.

"We're going to come back to this later, Pup," I say as I clear the last of the food from my throat. "I want the story on this conversion camp thing at some point, but first I think we need to cover what happened this morning."

Toby starts shaking his head animatedly. It doesn't take a genius to realize that the pup has been keeping the severity of the nightmares a secret from his best friend.

"What happened this morning?"

"I got locked out without a coat," Toby rushes to say and shoots me a glare. He doesn't want Shiloh to know about the night terror.

"You had a night terror, Shiloh," I say over Toby's rambling explanation about going out shopping, effectively cutting him off. "It was kind of intense. To be honest, if it wasn't for the fact that the buildings around here are all commercial buildings and closed at this hour, we probably would have had the cops called from your screaming."

Shiloh looks ashen. His head whips to Toby who is suddenly extremely interested in the crumbs left on his plate.

"How long have I been having the night terrors, Tobe?"

Toby shrugs and picks up his juice.

"How long?" Shiloh demands, making us both flinch. I haven't heard this tone from him in the time we've been cohabiting.

"You were getting better," Toby gets onto his knees facing his best friend. "You were so excited the first night you didn't wake up from a nightmare that I couldn't bring myself to tell you. You thought you stopped having them, but I just learned to calm you so you wouldn't wake up.

"I hated seeing you hurting after having them. I wanted you to be able to forget whatever hell that asshole put you through. Even though I knew you still went there in your sleep, I hoped I could let you have peace while you're awake."

The look of betrayal on Shiloh's face breaks my heart.

"I thought I was better!" he yells. "I became dependent on you because I thought you kept the damn memories away! You fucking used me!"

I can't stand to see these two men at odds with one another, so I open my mouth and bring both of their attention to me.

"What asshole?"

59

SHILOH

Toby never kept the nightmares away. He just let me think they were going away. He lied to me...for over a year. I fucking cut back on my therapy because of it!

"What asshole?" Don asks and I whip my gaze to him. I forgot he was here. I forgot the man who has taken care of me for the last month because my entire world just shattered at the realization that my best friend lied to me.

"How much do you know about how I came to end up at Kink Manor?" I ask him and he tells me Matt told him a little bit.

I nod in acknowledgment and steady my breathing. Not even Toby knows the full extent. He saw the way I was still limping when he moved in months after me. He knows my story is not a happy one, but he only knows what my nightmares revolve around. I've only ever given enough to explain away my reactions to things based on who I was when the guys found me three years ago. This will be the first time I'm telling anyone my story in its entirety, including the parts not even my therapist knows.

"My father died when I was three." The words pour out and I struggle to keep going. It's time to trust these men with my whole heart.

"Mama's parents helped us a little bit after that, but they both passed when I was four or five. I don't remember struggling financially, but we must have because two weeks before my sixth birthday, Mama surprised me by telling me she found me a new Daddy. That was the day she brought Frank to our home."

"He's a good man, Shy. You'll see. A boy needs a father."

My mother's words swirl around in my head. She said it enough times that I couldn't forget if I tried. I reach for my now tepid coffee and choke down a mouthful to wet my suddenly dry mouth. Why the fuck is this so hard?

"At first it was great having a dad. I mean, I was teased mercilessly at school for being raised by a single mother."

It feels weird when the smile starts to form on my face. The memories aren't *all* bad, but it's been a long ass time since I've let myself remember the good times.

"Frank would play catch with me. He took me to Pirate games in the summer and to my one and only Pens game that fall. He even took me to the Carnegie Science Center when they had the traveling dinosaur exhibit.

"But it all changed when we were at the mall and he ran into one of his high school buddies. I overheard them ask him who my real daddy was because let's face it, no one would ever assume my father is an almost seven foot tall Nordic giant. I didn't realize it then because I was just a kid, but that was enough to twist it in his mind that Mama and I humiliated him."

I turn my head to stare out my window. I know I'll never get through everything if I have to see their reactions. This is my deepest pain. Michael might have been abusive, but he never even tried to show me love. He was never family. Frank was the only father I had ever known.

"After we got home that day, he was always mad. Mama tried to cheer him up and make him happy, but he just drank more and more. I started to notice bruises on Mama when I would come home from school. She said she was just clumsy, but a part of me knew better, especially when she started to send me over to Mr. Jones's house more often."

My breath hitches and I focus on the hands that are gripping my thigh. I still can't look at him, but I know Toby has an idea of where things are going.

"One day, shortly after my seventh birthday, I skipped school and hid in the tree in Mr. Jone's backyard so that I could watch over my mama."

I pull my knees to my chest, dislodging Toby's hands. My eyes are no longer seeing the sprawling college campus outside of the window. All I can see is the old house with my neon green BMX bike thrown haphazardly on the lawn. I swear I can almost the smell of apples in the air from the bushels we brought back from Trax Farms the week before it all went to hell.

A hand grips the back of my neck and pulls me out of the memory. I meet Don's sympathetic eyes before resting my chin on my knees and recentering myself. I have to remember that I'm no longer alone. Even though nothing has been said, I know these two complete me and I'll fight every fucking day to keep them.

"Mama didn't fall like she always told me she did. I watched through the window and saw when Frank slapped her so hard she couldn't keep her feet. I remember he was screaming about her getting the wrong milk.

"I was in shock. He beat her. The only father figure I could ever know was hurting my mother. All because the store ran out of whole milk and she had to buy two percent for his coffee. I fell out of the tree which resulted in a broken wrist. But I didn't care about my own pain as I raced into the house. I remember screaming at Frank over and over to stop hitting my mother."

Daddy! Stop! Mama's crying! Please, Daddy Frank!

"At one point, I guess I threw myself in the way and got slammed into the cabinets hard enough to crack a few more bones and get a decent concussion. I was lucky, they said..."

The self deprecating chuckle that escapes brings a

tighter grip on my neck from Don and a whimper from Toby.

"Yeah, I was lucky alright. Lucky enough to be in so much pain that I couldn't move and had to watch as the only father figure I had ever known beat my mother beyond the point where she was no longer breathing. I watched as the light left her eyes because her terrified gaze never left me. I watched as her body jerked with every impact, long after she was already gone to heaven with the angels."

Glancing up from my knees, I want to stop. I want to sink into the comfort of forgetting again, but I need to get it all out. With a small shake of my head, I lick my lips to continue.

60

DONNIE

I'm going to kill Matt for being the fucking master of the understatement of the century. There's a big fucking difference between a kid watching his mother die and a kid watching his mother being beaten to death by his father because she bought the wrong milk.

"What happened next?" Toby asks quietly when Shiloh makes it clear that he doesn't want to sink into our comfort right now. I'll have to make do with keeping him grounded with my hand on his nape until he's ready for us to smother him with love.

"The police arrested Frank," he says like it's a no brainer. "The social worker at the hospital started searching for family members who could take me in, but it turns out that my mother was the only one listed on my birth certificate or my father who was listed wasn't really my father or something like that. Either way, there were no blood relatives able to be found.

"I should have gone into foster care, but my stepbrother was somehow granted temporary custody to start. I'd only met him once before when he showed up to demand money from Frank. I think I was still in shock because I didn't care who I went with at that point. I just wanted to get away from the police and doctors who kept looking at me like I was broken. I should have done more to stop Frank, but I didn't. My mama was gone and nothing else really mattered to me."

How do I get it through his head that it's not his fault. What could one little boy do against a grown ass man? He wasn't even supposed to be there.

As if he can read my thoughts, Shiloh looks up to meet my eyes and I get it now. Survivor's guilt doesn't make sense. It doesn't follow rational thought. I should know. I suffer through it every day. It's why I still won't set foot in any ice barn.

"If you remind me, I'll remind you," I whisper in his ear before he can continue his story. Shiloh gives me a small nod and a smile in acknowledgment. The little shit already knows. Well, now I feel dumb...

"Living at Michael's place wasn't all that bad at first. He grabbed my clothes and stuff from the house where I grew up so I wouldn't have to go back into that house. And his place was less than a block from the library which was nice. I spent a lot of time there with their after school programs and just reading to my heart's content."

He gets a sad look and ads, "I missed seeing Mr. Jones every day, though. So it was nice to see him again at your shop."

I move my arm across his shoulders and meet Toby's

eyes. He looks haunted like he knows what's coming and it isn't good.

"After a while, the social worker stopped showing up. I didn't realize until years later that he had either fooled them or bribed them enough to give him full and permanent custody. Frank ended up dying in custody before he ever went to trial, so no one knew anything about Michael or that he was virtually a stranger to me.

"See, Frank loved me in his own way. One of my therapists over the last few years pointed it out to me. It wasn't until people he deemed important made it clear that I couldn't be Frank's kid biologically that he began to change. He wanted a do-over on being a father, and the fact that I'm most definitely not white ruined his fantasy."

Well, fuck. Shiloh seems to have a better understanding of his traumas than probably anyone I've ever met. Never in a million years would I be willing to try and understand Rafe or any of those other asshole rapists. I might have loved Rafe like a brother once upon a time, but fuck seeing the good in him after the monster was revealed.

"Apparently Michael thought the same as my therapist because he was constantly complaining to me that he didn't understand how his father could love a ... ya' know... more than his own flesh and blood."

"I know you hate that word," Toby says as he moves his right hand to Shiloh's knee and leans his head against my hand on his shoulder. I lift my hand to run my fingers through the pup's hair. Shiloh swallows hard and nods before continuing.

"Once the time came for me to enter middle school, he moved us away from the home the social workers visited to the rat trap where I was until the day I escaped."

"Escaped?" Toby gasps out, almost falling off my lap. "What do you mean escaped? I thought the dickwad was arrested for what he did to you."

Shiloh shakes his head sadly and lets his arms flop to his sides.

"Eli told me that the district attorney's office claimed that they didn't have enough evidence to get him on the assault since I declined to press charges for it when I turned over the evidence for the drugs and everything else for the raid. Dunno how they didn't have enough considering the cops had to pull my bloody unconscious body down from his fucking house. He claimed he had no idea who did that to me, and they fucking believed him, like they always did."

Toby's gasp makes me realize I unintentionally fisted my hand in his hair. I hurry to release my grip and gently scratch his scalp in apology. I might want to inflict a little pain for pleasure, but I never want to give my boys pain out of anger.

"Long story short," Shiloh's voice interjects. "Michael had beaten me regularly from the time I hit middle school until I was taken to the hospital shortly after I graduated high school. I was there for two weeks before they kicked me out. I had healed up enough to satisfy the bare minimum standard of care and the charity that had been paying my bills had no more money for me."

"Eli spotted me as I was limping by McKinley's on my way back to that shithole the cops pulled me out of. I didn't have money for a ride and with it being a Sunday, the busses that I needed had already stopped running for the night. He pulled me inside the bar and before the night was over, I was given a room at Kink Manor."

61

DONNIE

It's been a little over a week since we had our twenty four hours of emotional blowout between the three of us. That morning, I had Jessica run the shop while we spent our time really getting to know each other better. Hearing all of the fun stories about their found family at Kink Manor makes me thankful that I got to know them at all.

The soft whoosh of the door opening makes me smile as Matt comes in for his mid-morning caffeine fix. I have to remember to thank Toby for so thoroughly destroying the damn bell at the beginning of the semester.

"The usual?" I ask the harried looking professor as he starts patting himself down frantically.

"Fuck! I forgot my wallet in my office," he says throwing his head back in exasperation. "Eric is planning three different Halloween parties and he's been driving me insane by insisting that we not only need to have couple costumes, but that each party needs a different costume."

Chuckling, I finish making his white chocolate mocha with an extra shot of espresso and double whipped cream. "Do you really care or is his stress giving you stress?"

He laughs as I hand over his drink. We both sit at my reserved table half hidden behind the counter and I yell for the new guy, Sid, to take over the counter if anyone comes in. I ran into him when I was finishing up my morning run a few weeks ago and he asked if I was hiring. I'm glad I gave him a chance because he has definite management potential.

"You know it's just him freaking out that's getting me all worked up," Matt tells me after taking his first sip. "It doesn't help that he just found out that after the holidays, his room at the manor house will officially have a new resident."

"You think he's regretting moving in with you?" I don't even try to hide the incredulity in my voice. If there was ever a perfectly matched pair of individuals, it would be Eric and Matt.

He gives me a smirk and rolls his eyes. "I'm pretty sure it's the fact that he loses that security net and it makes living with me real in a way that it wasn't before. Plus, I think he's afraid everyone in the house is moving on without him.

"Spencer is busy with Lucky. Shiloh moved in with you, and Toby might as well join him if the last week is any indication. My boy doesn't do well with big changes."

Matt and I spend the rest of his morning break discussing the Halloween party being thrown at Kink Manor. It's apparently going to be a pre-welcome party for the new resident before he officially moves in during the week between Christmas and New Year's Day. I have to admit, Eric really outdid himself with this one. I'm just lucky that I have a costume that fits the theme and won't have to go out shopping.

"I'll let him know you don't need his assistance with the costume," Matt calls out before disappearing out the door. Shaking my head, I head back toward my office to try and tackle some of the paperwork to see if I'm any closer to meeting the margins I need in order to secure the funding I need for the expansion. I'd love to turn Walt's Coffee Shop into a café and offer real food as an alternative to the restrictive hours and limited options of the dining halls.

"What the *fuck* did you just say to him?!"

Toby's angry shout has me jumping up from my desk and racing to the front. One thing I've learned over the last week is that my pup is very much a guard dog for those who he deems to be his people. He also has a tendency to act first and think later, so I hope I'm quick enough to stop him from killing a customer.

As I clear the corner, I'm shocked to see Sid holding a snarling Toby back from Jessica, my assistant manager. Taking a quick glance around the shop, the students who are in here are all regulars whose expressions range from smug to livid.

What the fuck have I been missing in my shop?

"It's not worth it," Sid is saying to Toby while struggling to retain his hold around the smaller man's waist. "I've been called worse. At least the guys in high school were creative in their bigotry."

Before I can say anything, Jessica snarls out, "I don't need a fuck toy fairy-boy to protect me from a boy who can't even stick to his own race. What's he gonna do? Sic his thug boyfriend and his gangbanger cousins on me?"

I see red. There's no fucking way that one of my employees, one of *Walt's* employees, could be so fucking hateful, but I can't deny what she just said. My eyes roam the shop and a few students meet my gaze. The looks on their faces show that this isn't a recent occurrence.

"YOU ARE FUCKING FIRED!"

My words cut through the tension and Toby stops fighting against Sid's hold to escape. All eyes in the room focus on me. Jessica looks smug while Sid looks like he's going to be sick as the silence lengthens after my outburst.

"Don't fire him," Toby runs up to me pleading. "I'm the one who yelled first. It's my fault."

I pull him into a hug and glare at Jessica over his head. "Sid isn't the one getting fired."

My manager blanches and has the gall to look surprised.

"I have been the manager since before Walt retired. I've been here for years!"

Ignoring her, I push Toby back to arms length to ask, "What exactly did she say to set you off, Pup?"

"I didn't say anything to your boy toy!" Jessica cuts in before he can answer me. "I know he and the rest of the trailer trash freaks are off limits."

Toby turns to face her and I'm almost too slow in stopping him from launching himself at her. Since I restrained his body, my pup takes a deep breath in preparation of what I'm sure would be scathing. Unfortunately, I don't think the dean will look past another incident with him, so I act quickly.

I barely have my hand over his mouth when Eric's voice from behind me has me struggling not to laugh out loud.

"Just cuz we get more cock in a week than you'll get in your life, Sour Patch Tits, doesn't mean you get a free pass to be a hateful bitch. If you're an example of what the hetero guys in this city have to choose from, I'm not surprised that the meat market for dick is having a booming expansion lately."

Jessica's scream of frustration makes me wish I had my hands free to cover my ears, but she at least takes off her apron and grabs her purse from beneath the counter. When she reaches the door, Eric steps aside with a wave of his hand.

She looks back at me with rage evident on her face, but I will never tolerate bigotry in my shop. I tell her that her last check will be mailed to her and that she is no longer welcome inside my establishment. I guess I'm taking another trip down to the security office on campus this afternoon.

62

TOBY

After the bitch exits the shop, the students who are hanging out start applauding. Jessica has been a real problem in here for a long ass time. It was practically torture when I was avoiding Owner for those weeks with having to deal with her bigoted ass. Now that she's officially gone, the rest of the students she drove away should start coming back.

Owner's arms loosen and I relax against his side. I'm not ready to move away yet. The whole reason I ducked in here after class instead of heading for the dining hall is because I was hoping for some snuggles. Shy's in deadline mode in the art building, so we won't see him until well after sundown for the next few days. Therefore, I came to Owner for some good pets.

"I'm sorry, Owner," I mutter into his shoulder. "I didn't mean to cost you your manager."

I really don't mean to fly off the handle, but when I saw her tearing down the new guy, I lost it and now

Owner is going to have even less time to play with me and...

FUCK!

We debated for hours the other night over the title that Don should hold with us as his pets. Like I pointed out the night he brought us both home from the club, we couldn't use *Master* without some well-meaning overly sensitive person throwing a hissy fit on Shiloh's behalf. So, we landed on Owner for when we're at the club or at home – and his shop is neither of those places.

"I mean... Fuck! Don! Shit..."

Lips press against mine and my brain short circuits before it can succumb to full blown panic mode. The tension in my body flows away as I sink into the bliss that is my Owner taking control.

Wolf-whistles from the customers in the shop break through my serenity and I jump back, almost falling over a stool in my excitement. Don just chuckles at the blush that I can feel heating my face.

"If I knew that's all it would take to shut him up, I might have tried that before Mattie showed back up in my life," Eric murmurs from somewhere behind me while I struggle to get my face back to a normal color.

"No you wouldn't," Donnie tells him and steps behind the counter to start tapping on the screen. "It would be too close to incest for you, and you know it."

While the two of them laugh at my expense, my eyes are drawn to the new guy staring at Eric. Even with Jessica spewing her venom, I've never seen him show any aggression or negative emotions. The worst I've seen on his face is annoyance or exasperation. He's an overall friendly guy and a ton of fun to talk to when it comes to menu planning for healthy, but tasty meals.

Right now, he looks like he can't decide if he wants to be happy or lose his lunch.

"Izzy?" he asks softly and Eric freezes mid-sentence with Owner before turning around to look at the new guy. "Do you remember me?"

Based on the look Eric is giving the poor guy, it looks like the answer to that question is a resounding "no" and I can't help but feel sorry for him. My friend spent a lot of time sleeping around before Professor Barnes came back into his life, and a lot of that time was used as a tool to forget some really bad shit that happened to him.

It was only a matter of time before one of Eric's conquests caught up to him, but this is really going to make things awkward for Owner having his new guy being a notch in our Brat Queen's bedpost.

"What's going on, Pup?"

Owner somehow snuck up behind me and is watching the show in front of us. "Do you know how Sid and Eric might know each other?"

Leaning back, I whisper in his ear my theory that the new guy, Sid, is likely one of Eric's former fucks based on the fact that he called him by another name. Eric never gave his real name out to anyone he was with. Usually, he told them his name was Alan, as a way to get them to scream his homophobic father's name out during butt sex.

"That can't be," Don whispers back in my ear while

Eric shakes his head at whatever Sid is saying. I can't really read the situation, but Eric hands the guy a business card before running out of the shop. Watching Sid pocket the card and return behind the counter to prep for the lunch rush, I turn to face Donnie and ask why he thinks that.

"He can't be a former lover for a couple reasons." He pulls me down on his lap at our hidden table in the corner. "First of all, Sid is from South Dakota and has only been in town for the last couple of months. You and I both know that there is absolutely zero chance that Eric has been with anyone else since he and his Mattie reconnected back in the spring.

"Secondly, Sid is only nineteen. He falls into the 'ick factor' as our favorite brat calls it. You know Eric gets skeeved out by thinking of anyone under twenty one having sex with someone older."

I let out a giggle that would make Lucky proud and can't seem to stop. Owner is looking at me like I've lost my mind, which of course only makes me laugh harder. It takes me for-fucking-ever to get under control, but somehow I manage it just as the rush finally starts to trickle in.

"Do I get to find out what's so funny before I have to go un-zombify the student population for the afternoon?"

I press a kiss to his cheek and push him toward the counter. I watch for a few minutes while he starts doing all the fancy barista shit before I walk up to the pick up area, snagging my regrettably decaf spiced apple latte.

Owner doesn't like me having caffeine between ten in the morning and three in the afternoon.

"See you at home after class?" he calls out in between orders as I gather up my stuff to head to my afternoon class. I nod and head toward the door. Halfway there, I turn and run back up to the counter to lean over to tell him what I forgot to say.

"By the way, I just turned twenty one at the end of August."

The clang of the metal cup hitting the tile and the hissing of the steamer wand precede the laughter of the entire shop when Donnie's ears turn bright red and I race out of there, cackling like a loon.

63

"Why the hell is the black man the skeleton?"

Eric taps my nose with his pinky and resumes painting my face for the Kink Manor Halloween party. I'm glad he knows I'm only messing with him. Out of the three different parties he has had to plan for the holiday, this is the one I was looking forward to the most.

"Hush up, Kitty-cat. You know Brook is your favorite Straw Hat," he tells me as he sponges more white makeup onto my face. "Plus, you have the natural afro so I didn't have to borrow one from Malcolm. That queen is way too stingy with his wigs."

I chuckle and reach up to feel the poof-ball that my natural hair reverts back to whenever I remove the braids. As soon as Donnie told me what the theme was for the party tonight, I rescheduled my appointment with Tara for getting my braids redone until after Halloween. She surprised me by *not* charging me extra for the schedule adjustment, but demanded photos once she heard what my costume was going to be.

Toby bounces into the room, and I have to laugh. I never would have put our precocious pup as the pervy chef, but oddly it fits. Not only does the blond hair and bubble but match perfectly, but unbeknownst to the rest of the guys, Toby's culinary skills are damn near divine. He's set to graduate from his program next week, and I couldn't be prouder of him. I don't know why he is still afraid to tell the rest of our family about culinary school, but I'm leaving the decision up to him.

"Only way you'd be more perfect for your character is if he liked taking a dick up his ass," I tell him when he sneaks in to give me a kiss when Eric steps out to grab another piece for my costume. "I hope our owner remembered to plug you good for later tonight cuz I really want to know what panties my pup is wearing."

A choking laugh comes from the doorway and I see Spencer shaking his head next to a guy I've never seen before.

"Daddy! I want to show Stan my playroom!" Lucky shouts from the top of the stairs leading to the top floor that he shares with Spencer. "You said I could show him when he got here and now he's here!"

The man who is standing with Spencer turns an interesting shade of red and makes that choking sound again before Daddy Spence smacks him on the back with a smile.

"Regretting it yet?" he asks the man who shakes his

head and returns the smile. Spencer looks at us before talking again.

"Shy, Tobe, this is Stanley Sinclair. He'll be moving in after Christmas since he managed to snag a decent job in town, but his mother is terrified of him living alone."

Stan throws an elbow into Spencer before facing us. "Call me Stan. After spending a month with this asshole traipsing all over Australia, I couldn't resist the lure of moving here and meeting all of the people featured in his tales from home. When he told me there was a vacant room in the house, I knew I had to take advantage of the opportunity. I'm just glad that there are more than just overbearing assholes like this guy living here."

Spencer puts him in a headlock in response and pulls him out into the hallway, both of them laughing the entire time. Eric scoffs and shakes his head when he passes them to come back and finish my makeup. Spence pushes his friend up the steps to his floor before coming back to the doorway.

"I wanted to show him the room he's gonna be moving into so he knows what to bring as far as furniture and stuff. Anything else you're taking beyond the vanity, E?"

Eric shakes his head and Spencer knocks twice on the doorframe in acknowledgement before racing up the stairs.

Neither Toby nor I will ever say a word about the tears that start to fall from his eyes as he continues to turn me into a living skeleton rock star for the party tonight.

64

TOBY

I put away the last of the breakfast dishes when my phone pings from the living room. I took it off silent after we finished eating. No phones at the table is probably the only rule from my childhood that I can see the benefit of.

Shiloh ran off to the studio to finish his midterm project for his sculpting class, and Owner is downstairs in the coffee shop going over some paperwork.

I still have another hour before I have to worry about getting to class. That's one of the huge benefits to me having practically moved in here. I'm no longer subjected to Spencer driving like a grandma and getting stuck on campus hours before I need to be.

Opening the Kink Manor group chat, I prepare myself for whatever fuckery they're up to now. It can't be too bad because most everyone should either be asleep, at work, or in class.

SparklesTheUnicorn:
@PanPup why the fuck did I get an invitation in the MAIL for a graduation ceremony for you??????

PanPup:
every1 shuld git 1

CaffeineDealer:
i think what my pup is trying to say is he's graduating from culinary school

AT THE TOP OF HIS FUCKING CLASS 🏆

he wanted to surprise all of u

Sad-die Eli:
Congrats, Toby 🎉🎉

AdorableAce:
Yay 4 Toby! 🎉

Does this mean you'll take over for Scotty?

Can I get brownies?

GamerSwitch:
If you ever want to cook something for the house LMK

when ur home that is

Holy shit! Scott is willing to let me in his kitchen to cook? The man is notoriously OCD when it comes to the main kitchen. He had to do a full replacement of the pots and pans when Eli accidentally scorched the bottom of a pan making a grilled cheese sandwich. One small scorch on the *bottom* of a pan, and he threw out the entire set. I'm pretty sure that set ended up going to Ash when they moved into their trailer.

SparklesTheUnicorn:
Like you'll ever let the ADHD pup operate anything in your kitchen beyond the microwave or toaster

We're all lucky you let us do that.

I have to say, that kinda hurts. Didn't he see that I'm fully certified and everything now? I can focus while cooking. It's one of the few things that I can always focus on.

GamerSwitch:
Had I known he was going to school for this, I'd have let him long ago

YOU on the other hand can burn water

so you need to stay TF out of MY kitchen

Sad-dieEli:
no fighting children

It's the landlord's kitchen

@SparklesTheUnicorn stop changing everyone's names in the house chat

SparklesTheUnicorn:

CaffeineDealer:
I was wondering how I got this name 🐾

VampireDaddy:
congrats @PanPup

i'll do my best to make it

i am invited right?

Caffeine Dealer:
the whole house is invited

plus the guys from the park... and the shop... and the club - BOTH clubs

each student got 10 tickets for the ceremony but he snatched up all the extras from his classmates that don't have as many family members

AdorableAce:
🍥 Kink Manor Commencement Takeover!!!!!

PrivateDickDaddy:
calm down little one b4 I put u in the corner

DAMNIT @SparklesTheUnicorn !!!

U don't even live in the house anymore

y do u still have chat admin privileges?

@SparklesTheUnicorn has left the chat

> **PanPup:**
> Not cool Daddy Spence

SuperMattie:
Prepare to grovel Spencer

ur lucky he loves you like a brother😒

AdorableAce:
UR A MEANIE DADDY

PrivateDickDaddy:
WTF?!

what did I do wrong this time?

***@AdorableAce has blocked
@PrivateDickDaddy from Kink Manor
Group Chat***

I jump out of the group chat because this is too much drama for me this close to class. I shoot Lucky a private message in the chat app instead of a text since I know he's on. He's supposed to be in class, so he's likely on his laptop and not his phone.

> **PanPup:**
> @AdorableAce u shuldnt blok ur daddy
>
> ur gunna git a spankin

AdorableAce:
I know 😅 but he doesn't understand how Sparkles feels about his room going to Stan

Daddy never had to know what it feels like to lose the only home you've ever known

he doesn't get what that room represents to Eric... or us

PanPup:
I'm worried about Eric

he seemed really sad at the party

AdorableAce:
he'll be ok

SuperMattie will keep him safe

I just need some duct tape to keep Daddy from making things worse

Wait... is it really duct tape? I always thought it was duck tape, like quack quack and feathers and all that stuff. I guess I learned something new.

The AI assistant device on the wall speaks up to remind me that I have fifteen minutes to get to class. Owner programmed my schedule into it last week and set it up to have the sexy Aussie accented dude remind me about my classes and all of my appointments. I shoot off one last message in the group chat to sign off and silence my phone.

PanPup:
u all wil eat 4 free opening my café

65

SHILOH

I've never been in the audience for a graduation ceremony. Hell, I was barely at my own high school graduation. I had to beg Michael for the money to rent the cap and gown for it and raced back to the house afterward to make sure that I was locked in by the time the sun went down. I learned at sixteen what happens when a young black man is out on the streets after dark in that neighborhood. Being detained by the cops for walking to the corner store for something to eat, I learned it's better to starve than be out after dark around there. Between the violence and the profiling, I vowed to never let myself get into that situation again.

"And now a few words from our top student this year, Tobias Grady!"

The announcement from the stage rouses my attention back to the auditorium and to my best friend, my lover, *my heart* standing behind a podium that makes him look so much more mature than the goofball I know and love. The roar of the crowd as we cheer makes everyone on the stage laugh.

There are only a little over a hundred graduates, and the venue for the commencement holds about a thousand spectators. Toby told us last night that they usually only fill about a quarter of the room for commencement since the pandemic, but we managed to pack the room almost completely full.

Obviously, all of Kink Manor has shown up, but our extended family came as well. All the people from the Manor Drive Mobile Home Park are here. All of our friends from the Monarch Room are here. Most of the puppies and kittens from the Devil's Club are here, minus the asshats that caused all the shit last time we were there. Even Don's employees are here, including the new guy, Sid and his roommate, Jesse.

"Today marks the end of a tough journey for a lot of us," Toby says into the microphone. "For those of you who don't know me, which I think is very few of the people here today from what I can see..."

The laughter that rolls through the audience brings a flutter of pride to my chest. I remember the boy who was desperate to blend in and fly under the radar when he first moved in. It didn't last very long, but I'm still proud that he's embracing his uniqueness now.

"I'm not exactly a person you'd expect to excel at something requiring the precision and attention to detail that the culinary arts demand. To say I have squirrel brain would be an understatement. But the kitchen is where my grandmother showed me I was loved growing up. The kitchen is where I learned that I was *not* a fuck up... Sorry Chef Reynolds."

Toby turns around to give a small wave and bow of his head to an older man sitting in the front row on the stage who is shaking his head in a way that pretty much anyone who has met our pup does on a regular basis.

"To cut to the chase, this school took a chance on this easily distracted, hyper kid and turned me into a chef. I think I can speak for my fellow graduates when I say it's been a privilege and a pleasure learning from all of the great chefs and restaurateurs who have dedicated their time to sharing their wealth of knowledge with us, the next generation. You took a chance and we will definitely make sure your gamble and sacrifice pays off. Feel free to come find me when I open my café in the future if you miss me."

Toby steps back from the podium and does this weird arm flourish thing and bows toward his instructors before turning back to the audience to throw his hands in the air in a victory pose.

"WE DID IT, BITCHES!!!!"

The auditorium erupts in laughter and cheers and my love runs and launches himself off the front of the stage. Owner and I both gasp in terror before the little shit becomes visible again among the crowd of his fellow graduates.

"This is one of the few times I wish he was taller," Donnie leans over to tell me. I know exactly what he means.

Fifteen minutes later, the ceremony is over and

everyone heads into the cafeteria where all of the instructors have prepared a buffet feast as a surprise for the graduates and their families. Before I even have a chance to let my eyes sweep the room, I'm practically tackled from behind by the love of my life.

"I'm so proud of you, Pup," Donnie ruffles his hair while I lean back to give him a kiss on his cheek.

"Thank you, Owner," Toby beams at us both and we get into line to sample all of the deliciousness in store.

"Tobias?"

Don and I turn to the unfamiliar voice, but Toby immediately stiffens in our arms. The woman in front of me is familiar in a way, but the way she's looking at us makes my hair stand on end.

"Don't ignore your mother, Tobias," she says and Don immediately steps in front of us both, shielding us from the wicked bitch of the deep south.

66

TOBY

No. No. No. No.

She can't be here. I didn't invite her.

How is she here?!

Today is supposed to be one of the happiest days of my life. *Why* does she have to ruin everything?

"You were *not* invited," Owner tells her. "You tried to destroy him. What the hell are you doing here? You should be back in your backwater shithole in Alabama. He specifically informed his father to tell you nothing about today. How the fuck did you know about this?"

Oh, fuck. Did my *father* invite her? I thought we were doing better. I forgave him for not standing up for me growing up. I trusted him with the invite for today.

Oh...Oh, God this hurts so much.

Shiloh's arms wrap around me and I can't stop the whimper that escapes at the thought of my father letting that woman back into his life, back into my siblings' lives. It's too late for me, but not them. She will destroy them all.

"Moira, what the hell are you doing here?" Uncle Robert's voice comes from behind me. "I thought I made it perfectly clear. You are never to show your face within a hundred miles of neither myself nor the man who you should have been proud to have as a son. Don't make me contest Mom's will because you and I both know that you and Janice can't afford that."

I turn around to see my mother and Uncle Robert glaring at each other on the other side of Owner. Shiloh keeps his arm around my waist, but gives me the freedom to choose how I want to react. My uncle's words remind me that I still have family who loves me and would never betray me.

"Proud? I should be proud of a pervert who has been corrupted by faggots and ni..."

"Finish that word, I fucking DARE you," I growl out as I turn toward the woman who, unfortunately, contributed fifty percent of my DNA. "Insult the men I love one more time and I don't give a fuck whose coochie I slid out of. I will knock your ass into the next decade Moira Grady."

Don's arm moves across the top of my back to grip my shoulder while Shiloh's grip on my waist tightens from the other side. Standing between the two men I love more than life itself, I face the woman who thought it was better to subject me to literal torture rather than love me for the person I was born to be.

"I am your *Mother*, Tobias! How dare you speak to me like that!"

Choking back my rage, I manage to respond through clenched teeth. "My mother died the moment she booked me a plane ticket to a conversion camp... Oh, I'm sorry. *Leadership retreat.*"

She stares at me with nothing but rage and contempt in her eyes. It feels like an eternity before she shrieks and storms out of the venue. At the sound of the door slamming closed, my legs give out and all control over my emotions evaporates. Sobs rip from my throat as Don gathers me up in his arms. I can feel us moving somewhere, but I can't bring myself to care.

Hours later, I wake up in our bed and can't really remember how I ended up here. We were supposed to be having a party after the banquet at Mr. Drag, but I guess my mother ruined those plans. I hope that everyone else got to party even in my absence. It's bad enough that I'm a genetic combination of a coward and bigot, but now I get to add delinquent and disturber of the peace to it as well.

Don's raised voice from the living room has me climbing out of bed in curiosity. Deciding clothing is probably in order if he's talking to someone, I pull on one of his gigantic hoodies that hangs midway down my thighs. I don't bother finding pants to pull on top of my boxers before heading to the hallway. Everything is all covered that needs to be.

I hear the shower running as I step into the hallway, so I guess that's where Shiloh is.

"He specifically told you not to let her know about tonight, Simon. She showed up... No, she didn't come to make peace with him. She fucking destroyed what should have been a highlight of his life... SHE MADE HIM FUCKING BREAK DOWN, YOU FUCKING ASSHOLE!"

Despite the fact that I have forgiven my father for being such a coward in my childhood, I can't deny the happiness I feel that my owner is making sure my sperm donor knows he fucked up today. I've never had anyone stand up for me like this — not since Me-maw.

Nothing could possibly stop me from crawling into Owner's lap right now, so I don't hesitate. Don merely switches the phone to his other hand to wrap his arm around me and pull my head down to his shoulder.

"If you weren't going to be coming, you shouldn't have said anything to them... That's fair, but it still falls to you. I'm not going to blame a seven year old for not understanding how her mother could hurt her big brother. I blame *you*, the parent..."

"Owner?" I hesitate to ask, but know this is something I need to do. "Can I talk to him?"

"Hold on, Simon," he says and pulls the phone down to his side. "Are you sure, Pup? You've been through a lot tonight. You can wait until tomorrow if you want. There's no rush to clear the air or let him off the hook."

"I need to get it out tonight, Donnie. It will fester if I don't. And I've given the pain they put me through enough of my time and energy."

Don kisses me on the forehead and hands me his

phone. Looking up, I see Shiloh come into the room wearing only his pajama bottoms. He takes a seat next to Don on the couch and grabs my other hand in support.

"Dad?" I hate the way my voice is so scratchy from earlier, but a part of me is glad he gets to hear what that woman put me through. He can't hide from it this time. "You still there?"

"Tobias, I am so sorry," he stammers. It sounds like he's trying not to cry, too. My father never cries. Hell, he barely smiles. I think the most emotional I'd ever seen him was the day he put me on the plane to come here.

"Rachel didn't know better. She told your mother she was mad that she couldn't go see you for your graduation party and that woman managed to get enough information out of her to find you. The court official didn't mention it to me. They're supposed to tell me if she talks to them about you or if she starts spewing her hate. I didn't even know she left Alabama until Robert called and ripped me a new asshole an hour ago."

There's a lot to unpack in that, but the loving gazes of my men help to keep me from spinning out. The thing that sticks with me is the fact that the woman can't even see her other children without supervision, lacking though it is. More than likely, the official didn't think anything of a seven year old complaining to their mother about not being able to go to a party.

"I don't blame you," I tell him after a pause. "I know you guys couldn't come because Richie got covid from his peewee football team. I especially don't blame

Rachel. I get why she was upset. She's a seven year old who was going to go on her first plane ride and see her big brother who she hasn't seen in three years.

"I was disappointed to not get to see you guys as well.

"I'm glad in a way that you weren't here. They don't need to see their mother the way I saw her tonight. Even knowing the monster was always there after the fact, tonight obliterated all the good memories. I don't want that for them."

I feel the tears start to fall again and I wonder how the fuck there's still any moisture in my body to still be able to come out.

"Tell me how to make it up to you, son," my father begs on the other end of the call.

Shiloh hands me a bottle of water and I glance at each of the men who hold my heart in their hands. I give them each a small smile and tell my father the only thing that matters at this point. His relationship with me has been damaged by today's events, but he can do better for my siblings.

"Make sure Richie and Rachel know you love them and will protect them *no matter what*," I say with a hitch in my voice. "Love them unconditionally and make sure they know it. Don't assume they know like you did with me. *Tell them*. Show them. Keep that bitch and her hateful relatives away from them.

"Don't let them suffer like I did."

I barely whisper that last part and hear my father's

gasp on the other end of the call. My heart can't handle anything else without another crack forming, so I thrust the phone back at Owner. I stop paying attention to whatever he's saying to my father and bury my face into his neck to let the tears fall.

67

SHILOH

It's two days before Thanksgiving and I don't know what the fuck to do to snap Toby out of this funk he fell into after his graduation and showdown with his mother last week. With the campus closing after classes finish today, Don and I are planning on heading back to Kink Manor to stay through the weekend in Toby's room. Considering the rent is paid up through the end of the year, Eli said the landlord doesn't need to know whether Toby is staying here or there.

My phone pings with the notification for the house group chat, so I open it up. I have it set to only notify me if someone tags me because Lucky has been spamming the chat lately with his letters to Santa. It's adorable, but seventeen different wishlists over the span of an hour is a little much.

GamerSwitch:
@ShyKitten are you guys still planning on coming over for Thanksgiving?

AdorableAce:
Shy Shy you HAVE to

I haven't seen you in FOREVER

DaddySpencer:
don't let him guilt u into coming

he just wants more people to push his santa agenda

AdorableAce:
DADDY!!!!!

ur not supposed to tell them!

I have to smile at their antics. Spencer finding Lucky, or rather Lucky stumbling upon us, was probably the best thing to ever happen to Kink Manor, or hell, Manor Drive as a whole. Him discovering his little side has brought so much light and laughter and love to all of us in the last year. I hope it continues.

GamerSwitch:
as cute as you are @AdorableAce there was a reason I was asking

is the pup still planning on helping me cook? if not, I gotta get started soon to get it all taken care of

PanPup:
I'll cook

lemme order a uber 2 cum over

> **ShyKitten:**
> @PanPup just come to the shop after class
>
> Owner is closing up as soon as classes r done 2day
>
> we r planning on staying at KM thru the weekend. did u 4get?

PanPup:
k

I run to the restroom so that Don doesn't notice the tears that I can't hold back anymore. I'm not sad as much as I'm fucking livid. That bitch broke my sweet and happy Toby and just flew back to Hicksville, Redneck Country to let the people who love him pick up the pieces. At least when she was shipping him off before, she didn't say anything.

Splashing water on my face, I check out my reflection in the mirror and decide it's good enough. If nothing else, it will look like I had a panic attack again. They're not as common as they used to be, even if they still happen way more often than I wish they did.

When I get back to my table, I notice a new text message alert.

Mr. Jones:
You and your men are welcome to join us
in Florida for the holiday if you would
like.

He attached a photo of him with his granddaughters
posing in the middle of a game of mini golf. I'm so glad
he's happy and not lonely anymore. I always worried
about him so much after I went to live with Michael.

Me:
Enjoy the sunshine with the girls. My
guys and I already have plans

Mr. Jones:
Tell Donald to close the damn shop and
go get your freak on until the campus
opens up on Monday morning

I damn near choke on my hot chocolate and Don
looks over in alarm. I wave away his concern with my
phone while I mop up what I spit onto the table with
some napkins.

Me:
MR. JONES! 😊

Mr. Jones:
Dad went to the restroom. This is Becca.
We all want you to be happy Shy

Me:
Thanks, Bex. Happy Thanksgiving

Mr. Jones:
 u2

"You alright?" Don's voice startles me and I look up to see the shop is empty. He's even sent Sid home, and I know that guy doesn't have anywhere to go. Something happened back home for him, and his family understands and isn't pushing him to come back. His dad was here a few weeks ago with his youngest siblings to go to a hockey game as a family, so I know the issues aren't related to his parents.

"Did you invite Sid to Kink Manor for Thanksgiving?"

Don chuckles at my attempt to change the topic, but he nods. "He already made plans to go with Jesse to his family's house up near Youngstown."

"That's good," I mutter and Donnie's brow furrows in concern while I stare at my phone. I can't stop worrying about our pup and what we could possibly do to help him move forward from the shit his mother pulled.

68

DONNIE

That might not have been the *most* awkward Thanksgiving dinner I've ever been at, but it certainly was uncomfortable. To say it was an unwelcome surprise for everyone to see Toby that subdued would be a massive understatement.

The food that he and Scott prepared was undoubtedly phenomenal Toby smiled when he was complimented, but it's glaringly obvious that his light is still dim after that bullshit his womb rental pulled a couple weeks ago.

"Why don't you guys head to bed?" Eli suggests when I bring our plates upstairs to the kitchen. The basement is the only place in the house with enough space to fit everyone other than outside, so that is where the actual meal was held. The theater room was converted into a melgamesh of hodge podge furniture and table settings. After the meal, I left my pets downstairs to relax while I came up to fret.

"He needs someone to pull him out of this, whatever it is." My frustration is palpable as I look to Eli for an answer. But the damn sadist just shrugs in response.

"This is probably the first time Toby has ever let any of us see him as anything other than the happy go lucky energetic pup — at least for longer than the length of a movie. I think it's a good thing he's showing us this side of him," he explains as he starts to fill the sink with hot soapy water. "You gave him a safety net. You gave him a home where he doesn't have to fear how he is perceived. You gave him a safe haven to let go and actually feel the bad stuff, to stop hiding it away from everyone who loves him. You're good for him, Don. You're good for both of them."

Eli leaves the hot water in the sink and heads for the stairs to the upper floors. I don't really understand why he wasted the water without putting any dishes in, but I was specifically instructed by no less than five people to not attempt to clean anything in the kitchen here on pain of death.

"Owner?"

I turn toward the basement stairs to see my boys standing in the doorway. It hurts to hear Toby so uncertain, but I hold my arms open for him. I'll always be open to him, to them both. He rushes into my arms reminding me of the excitement he used to always show for my hugs, before that woman showed up in our lives.

"Can we go home tonight?" he asks softly. My heart does a little happy jump at his calling my apartment his home.

"I did enough people-ing today. I don't think I have two more days of playing nice in me."

Shiloh gives me a small nod from across the room before he heads upstairs to pack our things. I lean down to kiss the top of my pup's head before I answer.

"Of course we can go home. Did you want to say goodnight to anyone before we leave?"

He shakes his head, so I keep hold of him as we head to the foyer to get our shoes on. Shiloh meets us there and tells me that he explained everything to Eli so we shouldn't have to worry about any freak outs in the group chat from the rest of our friends.

The drive home is eerily silent, enough to set my teeth on edge by the time I park in my spot behind the shop. When we enter the apartment, Toby heads straight for the bathroom. I worry that the big gathering might have been too much for him, too soon. The sound of the shower reassures me that he won't hear how pathetic I'm about to be as I turn to our other love in desperation.

"I need some fucking assistance here, Kitten. What the fuck do we do to help him?"

Shiloh joins me on the sofa, mirroring my own help-lessness in his suddenly glassy eyes. "I have no idea, Donnie. I have no fucking clue and it's breaking my heart seeing him like this."

Neither of us notice the shower cutting off, but we hear the creak of the bathroom door. When the sound of his shuffled steps lead into the bedroom, I stand up and help Shiloh back to his feet as well. We need to go hold our pup. As long as it takes, I won't give up on him and I know Shiloh feels the same way.

69

TOBY

I've been numb for weeks. As bad as my womb shooter hurt me, it was my father that made me like this. Deep down, I never expected Moira Grady to change her tune. But I had already let my father back into my heart, and he trampled it. It doesn't matter that it was unintentional. It doesn't matter that he apologized after the fact.

He broke my trust. *He broke my fucking heart.*

Parents are supposed to love and protect their children. If someone who is supposed to be biologically conditioned to love me can't manage to do it, how the fuck am I supposed to believe that I can trust my heart to these men?

Shy would never hurt you like that. Owner stood up for Eric when he didn't even know him and had everything to lose. Neither of them would put you through what they did.

Shut up, stupid inner voice!

Logically, I know I can trust them. I know I can trust the guys at the manor. But my heart doesn't trust my brain right now. My heart is still stuck being the little boy who wants his mommy and daddy to love him. That little boy has been disappointed since his Me-maw died and left him alone in that family.

I can't keep doing this.

The people who gave me life don't have any more say in what I do with it. The only people who matter are the ones who have stuck beside me for the last three years — or three months in Owner's case.

The fact remains that he's been here and has fought for me even when he had zero clue who I was.

The knob for the shower doesn't squeak for once when I turn it off, and I have to smile at that. Sid told me a trick for fiddling with the way I turn it to stop the squeal. I didn't think it would work. Apparently, he had a lot of reasons to get very handy over the years as the oldest of five with two working parents.

Wiping the steam off the mirror, I am shocked by my appearance. I've been avoiding looking at myself since my graduation. I've been avoiding a lot.

Running my hand over the scruff on my cheek, I realize I look like absolute shit. A beard is most definitely not in my future, but the smile feels like it's the start of something new. I'm determined to make it work with the men I love.

Tonight is our fresh start.

It doesn't take them long to join me in the bedroom after I finished having my epiphany. I can't stop the smirk from showing on my face at the looks on their face.

The fact that I'm laying naked in the middle of our bed is apparently a bit of a surprise for them.

I'm done hiding behind the fear. I'm going to be brave and fight for what I want, for those I love.

"It's good to see you smile, Pup," Owner rumbles as he pulls off his shirt and climbs onto bed next to me. "How do we make it stick around?"

I feel Shiloh press against my back while I stare into our owner's eyes. The pain in them is something I need to remedy. I put that there.

SHE put that there.

Okay, inner voice is kinda smart tonight...

"Just love me," I tell him and lean forward to press my lips to his. Shiloh's arms wrap around me from behind and I hand the bottle of lube to my owner. "Show me how much you love me tonight. I need my Owner. Own me. Both of you."

I hold my breath until I feel a hand wrap around my cock and slowly start to stroke it. Looking down, I love to see the contrast of Shiloh's dark to my light as my cock disappears into his fist over and over again.

"I will love you forever if you let me," Don whispers, brushing his fingers through my damp hair. I tear my eyes away from Shiloh's hand on my dick to look at the man who owns me heart and soul. Well, the pieces that Shiloh hadn't already claimed at least.

"I love you, too" I gasp out as Shiloh squeezes a bit tighter and pulls his hand away. "I love both of you so much and I'm sorry I struggled to show it the last few weeks."

Before I can turn around to look at my best friend when he pulls back, Owner grabs my chin and forces me to look at him instead. The snick of a bottle cap registers too late for my brain to realize what is happening. By the time it catches up, Shiloh is already pressing against my asshole.

"It's going to be tight, but I don't have the patience to do prep tonight, Tobe. I love you too much to hurt you, but I need you too much to wait. Tell me you're okay with this, pup."

I can't bring myself to say the words, but Don seems to understand. He sees it in my eyes what I can't make my mouth say and nods to our lover to continue. He reaches down to resume stroking me slowly to help ease the burn of Shiloh's entering me.

Time stretches on for what seems like forever as Shy slowly pushes inside while our owner lazily strokes me off.

It burns.

It hurts.

Donnie's eyes never leave my face, tracking every flicker of emotion that races across my features.

It feels amazing and wonderful and torturous all at the same time. My body can't decide if it wants to stop or never surrender. I want to freeze like a statue and thrash like a wild beast. It's amazing and terrifying and I can't stop the tears from falling.

"Let it go, Toby. You can let go. We'll always catch you."

Owner's words are the final push I need and my

orgasm crashes over me. I taste blood in the back of my throat from the force of my howl, but I let it all drift away on the bliss I feel seeing the men I love smiling down at me.

I don't want to close my eyes, but eventually exhaustion wins out.

70

SHILOH

The last day of the semester is always bittersweet, but this time I feel like it's transformative. For the first time since I was a kid, I'm looking forward to Christmas. Toby has officially moved into the apartment with us, and we turned my old room into an office for Don and a studio for me.

I'm going to miss having access to the full art building for the next three weeks, but at least I can paint and sketch in the apartment. It was always too busy at Kink Manor to get enough down time to really let go creatively. My downtime was usually spent in kitten space in the basement if I got any.

"All done for the year, Kitten?" Don comes around the counter to greet me with a kiss before I take my usual seat at our table. I nod as he heads back to help Sid clear the unexpected rush of students. They all seem to be needing a last minute caffeine fix before hitting the roads.

It doesn't hurt that most of the professors canceled classes to give the out of town students the opportunity to beat the winter storm they're calling for tonight. Days like this make me glad I took the loan offered by the old landlord to be able to come here for school.

"Toby should be here soon," I tell him as I pull out a sketchbook to mess around with the logo for the café they want to build together. "He wanted to drop something off to that Greg guy before he left to head home. I guess he's graduating early and Toby still feels bad about the fight back in the beginning of the semester."

The blast of cold air from the door makes me shiver before I turn to see who was asshole enough to push the door open that wide. I freeze in place as I lock eyes with my worst nightmare in the flesh.

"DONNIE!" I scramble out of my seat and race behind the counter in terror. Don grabs me by the shoulders and pushes me behind him to face down the demon that destroyed me.

"You need to leave," Sid growls out while I hide behind my owner. I've never been so thankful that Toby is late. He would attack Michael and then I would lose him. Don and Sid could probably take him eventually if they worked together, but my best friend would be snapped like a twig.

"I just want to drop this off. You'll never see me again." Michael's voice sounds different, softer, from what I remember, but then again, monsters are always worse in our dreams and memories. "For what it's worth, I'm sorry Shiloh. I fucked up both of our lives all because of a bastard who cared more about his image than being a decent human being."

The woosh of the door and blast of cold air isn't enough for me to accept that he's left. I keep my eyes squeezed shut, hiding as much as I'm able behind the man I love, but when Don turns his back to the door, I know we survived my worst nightmare.

"I can handle this solo for a bit," Sid says as I bury my face into my owner's chest. I can barely stay upright from the crash of adrenaline. "Why don't you guys head to the office for a bit? I'll send your pup back when he gets here."

Donnie thanks his employee and pulls me down on the futon in his office, wrapping his arms around me tightly while I feel like I'm vibrating out of my skin. It could have been minutes or hours, but eventually the shaking stops and I don't feel like the world is shattering around me anymore.

"Do you want to read the letter now or wait for Toby to get here?"

I didn't even notice a letter next to Don on the futon. Where did it come from?

"I just want to drop this off..."

Oh.

He wrote me a letter. "I didn't realize monsters could write."

Don's chuckle makes me realize I said that last part out loud. In the end, I decided to wait for Toby to get home and for us to close the shop and go upstairs where I can fall apart safely in the arms of the men I love.

While Toby is understandably upset to have not been there when the source of all of my nightmares showed up, the look I share with Don assures me that he agrees with me that it was a good thing our pup was preoccupied when Michael showed up. I'm still debating calling the cops for him violating the restraining order, but I've decided to read the letter before I make any type of decision on sending his ass back to prison.

"Time to rip off the bandage, Kitten." Don hands me the letter after we finish dinner.

I don't want to read it, but I feel like I owe it to that seven year old boy to find out why the fuck he had to grow up and suffer like he did. Ripping open the envelope, I feel Toby's arms snake around my legs from his seat on the floor. Don lays his arm across my shoulders and reads along with me.

Dear Shiloh,

I'm not good at a lot of things, especially making amends. They say it's an important step in rehabilitating me for society. Going into this program, I only looked at it as a way to reduce my sentence and get out to make you suffer for turning me in.

I'm not going to lie to you. I hated you when you put me in prison. Yeah, I knew that day that you went to the cops. I offered you to Bill because he was the one who gave me the heads up.

You weren't supposed to choose the cross, little brother. You were supposed to disappear with Bill and the cops would lose their case.

In a way, you earned my respect that day, and I will regret it for the rest of my life.

I swore after escaping my father's clutches, I would never be afraid of another man. But I was afraid of you from the second I met you. You had everything I once had. You had the loving mother and my dad adored you. I knew how it twisted me when shit hit the fan and I kept waiting for it to happen to you.

I took custody of you to be able to use you. I was just waiting for you to be just as fucked up as I was so that I could use you as an enforcer or to infiltrate some rival drug dealers turf. But you stayed so fucking pure. The more you kept out of my business, the worse I had to treat you to justify it in my fucked up mind that I still had worth.

I guess it all boils down to the fact that I was a self centered asshole and you NEVER did anything wrong to deserve what I did to you. If I could go back, I would leave you with the social workers.

I can't change the past, but please don't ever think you deserved what I put you through, what that drunk put you through. Your mom was a nice lady. I'm sorry she ever met my dad. I'm sorry she died.

If you're still reading at this point. I gotta say I always knew you would be a better man than me. I'm leaving town as soon as my parole officer can clear me for a transfer. I need to be away from this city. I need the fresh start and you don't need to be looking over your shoulder for me. You'll never see me again.

This is the only gift I've ever given you, and I'm sorry it is about fifteen years too late.

-Michael

PS ~ If there is ever anything I can do for you, I'm at your disposal. My parole officer will know how to get in contact with me.
I don't expect you'll ever want to even think about me again, but I would spend the rest of my life as a worm under your feet if it meant I could take back even the smallest fraction of the pain I inflicted on you in my misguided transference of my own.

Setting the letter on the coffee table, I can't help but shed a few tears for the relationship that never had a chance to develop between my stepbrother and I. There isn't a snowball's chance in hell that I will ever forgive what he did.

He was right. He is shit at making amends. But there is a sincerity in his written words that I never once heard from him in the decade he kept me with him.

"Are you alright?"

I look down into Toby's face and give him a soft smile.

"I think I am. I'm with the two men I love most and my nightmare is leaving town for good. I think for the first time in a very long time I am looking forward."

Don gently turns my face to him and asks, "Looking forward to what, Kitten?"

"Everything, Owner. I'm looking forward to everything."

EPILOGUE
TOBY

April

Loading the last of my stuff into the back of Eric's truck, I'm glad that the rain they predicted for the weekend held off. I didn't want to have to make multiple trips using Owner's sedan to haul everything.

"Is that everything?"

Think of him and he shall appear.

"Yes, Owner. The room upstairs is completely empty now and ready for the next person who needs to find their kink family." Pushing up on my toes, I press a kiss to Don's cheek before I rush off to join the others in the basement for the end of movie day. Don and Matt were voluntold by Eric that they are responsible for his truck and need to finish moving my stuff up into the apartment.

I didn't tell Owner, but the investors I found for our café are the guys from Kink Manor. Eric, Lucky, and Eli each have more money than they know what to do with.

The rest of us might be working class guys, but we're family. We've never let money get between us.

My phone pings with an alert to let me know I have a new text message.

ShyLove:
I have finished the preliminary logo. what do you think?

THE MUG SHOT

3 HOTS & A SHOT
OF EXPRESSO

Me:
I think The Mug Shot is gonna be a hit

A noise from the back porch distracts me from heading downstairs. Pushing open the screen door, I'm surprised to see Jace wiping hurriedly at his eyes before putting the lid on the trash can. He gives no indication that he sees me before he lumbers off to the back of the garage to disappear inside.

Me:
Something's wrong with TB

ShyLove:
y do u say that?

I lift the lid on the trash can and gasp at what I see. The bear that Jace has had his entire life is laying on top of the pizza boxes from earlier today. I snatch him off the pile of trash and brush him off as best I can. I don't know what the hell is going on with my friend, but one thing I know for certain. Anything that could convince him to throw out Sox is not something that he needs to have in his life.

> **Me:**
> I'll tell you at home. we need to safeguard a teddy 4 a bit

> **ShyLove:**
>

The sound of Jace's motorcycle spraying gravel against the garage wipes the smile from my face. I really hope whatever is wrong can be fixed for him.

"Come on, Sox. Shy and Donnie will help me take care of you until your little buddy is feeling better." Tucking the bear carefully into my backpack, I hope I'm not lying to him or myself.

ABOUT THE AUTHOR

I am a dog mom living it up in the insanity that is Northeast Ohio. When I'm not documenting the exploits of the characters in my head, I'm either binge reading the works of other amazing authors or losing my voice at hockey games. I'm horribly addicted to coffee, anime, and Asian dramas in addition to building my ever-growing stuffie army.

Kate Bauer is the contemporary alter ego of K.A. Bauer. I guess you could say Kate lives in this reality while K.A. is in a reality where mythical creatures and magic exist, and fate makes finding true love easier. All of her stories are LGBTQIA+ centric, and the characters fight for their rights and happily ever afters.

For the latest news on releases and appearances, check out my website www.authorkabauer.com and sign up for my newsletter.

I can be found on most social media sites under the username @authorkabauer

MORE BOOKS BY
KATE BAUER

MANOR DRIVE SERIES

A Little Discovery

Drag Me Up

Pet Project

Teddy Tea Time

Night Shift

No Pain, No Gain

UP/DOWN SERIES

Stood Up

Let Down

Trade Up

Down Play

Up For Promotion

WRENSHAW UNIVERSITY SERIES

Freshman Fifteen

Injured Reserve

Professor's Pet

Too Many Men

Dean's List

Frequent Flier

BOOKS BY
K.A. BAUER

ALPHA'S LITTLE PSYCHO SERIES

Alive

Holly Jolly Psycho (Novella)

Unburied

Afraid

Complete Series Omnibus

JAMESON PACK SERIES

Doctor Mate

Fated Mistake

Half Mate

Learned Fate

AFFILIATED STORIES NOT INCLUDED IN SERIES

Fated To Be Free

FRESHMAN FIFTEEN

SNEAK PEEK
ADVENTURES IN TOY LAND

After freeing myself from fast food hell – thank you, kinky boss-man – I can finally focus on my goals for the year. When it comes to my schoolwork, I'm golden. Technically, I could have tested out of most of the entry level courses, but I decided to just take the courses in order to make sure I can acclimate to college life so far away from home. Dad wanted me to test out to be able to graduate early, but I want to live my own life and not stand out too much.

One thing I need to do is get something to prepare for when I do meet someone. I mean, I've played with myself before – what teenage boy hasn't? But from what I've looked up, there's a lot more preparation that is needed than me doing a reach around with my fingers. Plus, I can't quite manage to find my own prostate. It's not that I don't know where it is. I know basic anatomy. The issue is trying to find the opportunity to have enough time alone to truly explore it all.

"Where are you headed after work today, Sid?" Lucky – one of Toby's friends and a café regular – asks me after pulling out a coloring book when he sits at his usual table. He's another interesting person that I've met since starting as a barista. His boyfriend graduated last year but still shows up pretty regularly since he's friends with the boss-man.

"Maybe you can help me out," I answer and place his hot chocolate on the table. "You've lived here all your life, right?"

He nods and takes a sip of his cocoa while I ignore the angry huff from Jessica at the counter. That woman tried hitting on me during my first shift last week, but I made it crystal clear that I am not interested. Despite my verbal answer telling her that I am only attracted to men, she tried to cop a feel. At that point, I threatened to call the cops on her for sexual assault – in front of some customers – and she finally got the point that I am strictly dickly when it comes to my sexual attraction.

"So, if a guy was looking to get something to spice up his alone time, where would be a good place to go?"

While I had prepared for confusion or embarrassment, the outright giggle fest coming from the man is unexpected. With a frown, I head back behind the counter so that the bitch can take her damn vape break. It took days for me to get up the courage to ask someone. Maybe by Christmas I'll muster up enough to ask someone else.

I shouldn't have worried though. When my shift

ends, Toby and the boss-man are there to give me a lift to a store run by one of their friends.

"Sorry about Lucky," Don says after helping Toby into the backseat of his car. "He's ace, so the fact that you asked him about where to find sex toys cracked him up."

I climb into the passenger seat and wait for the boss-man to pull out onto the road before voicing my questions.

"Isn't he dating your friend?"

Toby laughs from behind me before answering, "Yeah, Lucky is Ace as fuck, but him and Daddy Spence are madly in love."

"Sex and romance are two completely different things for some people," Don says from beside me. "Spencer and Lucky have probably the most pure and loving relationship I've ever seen, but they aren't sexual. If you have more in depth questions, you'll have to ask them, but they've given us all blanket permission to explain that much when anyone asks."

"Yeah cuz Daddy Spence is fucking tired of people thinking Lucky is broken or that they don't love each other just cuz they don't suck each other off at every opportunity like we do."

"TOBIAS!"

My laughter can't be held back for the rest of the drive to the shop.

"This is a book store," I say when we climb out of the car in front of Sally's Adult Book Store. The only response from the others is laughter while they hold the door open for me.

As each of us crosses the threshold of the doorway, a chime sounds from the room behind the beaded curtain in the back of the room. Surrounding us are bookshelves – empty bookshelves. My confusion mounts as the guys head straight for the curtain and just walk on through. I follow them, but only because this dark room full of empty shelves is extremely creepy.

What I see beyond the curtain is something my brain cannot compute. There's a guy in a gamer chair playing on his phone sitting behind what appears to be one of those glass cases you see at stores where they lock up the valuable video games and cigarettes. I'm not even able to get a good look at the contents of the case before Toby is dragging me down an aisle.

There's something oddly horrifying about seeing things that your brain is trying to convince you could not exist in real life. Feather boas are hanging next to what looks like riding crops. And...

Okay, there is no fucking chance a human being could ever fit THAT. I freeze in horror at the thought of someone actually trying to stuff themselves – or God forbid someone else – with a three foot long glow in the dark replica of what I'm pretty sure is a horse penis. I've been on a farm and have *seen things*.

"Yeah, no. That's a gag prop for bachelorette parties," Don chuckles before pulling me to another aisle, leaving Toby to peruse the collection of leashes and collars displayed nearby. "If you're looking at getting something for yourself, my pup is not the one to be leading you around."

Still contemplating the physical impossibilities of the glow in the dark horse dick, I barely hear anything that my boss is saying while he explains the items in front of us. I've heard of dildos, plugs, and vibrators. What the fuck are these beads and why would anyone want to use them?

"Just remember if you get these, take them out slowly. It's not like trying to start a lawnmower. That would be a fast track to the ER."

Glancing towards the front of the store, the guy behind the counter sends a smirk in our direction before getting up to help the lady who just came in. Thank heaven, he is the only witness to my mortification at getting a sex toy education by my boss.

"Owner?"

Don rolls his eyes and laughs before excusing himself to track down his boyfriend while I try to not look absolutely lost and naïve. I need to choose something or else this trip will be a total waste that I will never live down. I randomly grab a box showing three basic silicone plugs on the front.

Training Plugs: Increase your hole's elasticity.

I mean, I guess this fits the bill. Instead of stretching out the decision – no pun intended – I hustle up to the counter to check out. I can hear Toby and Don negotiating further back in the store and want to avoid the whole situation of my boss knowing what sex toy I decided to grab.

"I'll need more bullets," the lady in front of me says

to the clerk. "And something with a handle. I couldn't find anything on the shelf."

A handle? Bullets? Does she know what kind of a store she's in?

"I'm sorry, what?" The guy behind the counter looks just as confused as me. That isn't right. There's no way someone who works at a store selling sex toys should be as puzzled as the virgin who didn't even know before today that animal based dildos were a thing. And how does anyone know what a dragon cock would look like?

"The bullets keep getting lost in my husband's ass, so I was hoping to find something with a handle so that I don't have to dig them out."

Erp... Did I just hear what I just heard?

I look behind me to see Don struggling to hold in his laughter while keeping a tight grip on Toby, hand clamped over the younger man's mouth. Turning back to the front, the guy behind the counter is starting to turn a delightful shade of pink while he rings up the woman's purchase of three small vibrators, a box of peach flavored condoms, and six different bottles of lube.

I'm on another fucking planet...

A LITTLE
CHRISTMAS! JOHNNY

SNEAK PEEK
DEXTER

From mid November through the beginning of January is fucking retail hell. For the last few years, I managed to snag temp jobs to carry me through without having to resort to working with the public during this time of the year. Unfortunately, with the uptick in the number of companies using artificial intelligence to scrape resumes for their human resources departments, it has become more and more difficult to land a decent job without a college degree.

My parents' accident happened during my sopho-more year, and I was never able to go back after that winter break ended. I remember getting off the plane that morning and the notification of a voicemail on my phone. My parents had dropped me off at the airport for my red-eye flight back to Seattle the night before. At first, I didn't understand why a hospital in Pittsburgh was calling for me. I thought maybe one of my buddies from high school had listed me as their emergency contact so that they wouldn't get into trouble with their parents or something. Thankfully, I waited until I got back to my dorm room to call the hospital back because I fell apart. Everything after that was a blur. I know my RA helped me pack up and get back home. He even shipped all of my other things home when it was confirmed that I wouldn't return for the spring semester. Things came back to me later, after the funerals.

Dad died instantly. The doctors said he had a heart attack from the rush of adrenaline combined with the shock caused by all of his injuries. Mom somehow managed to hold on long enough for me to come say goodbye. I couldn't bring myself to go back to life as a college student despite their life insurance policies ensuring that there was enough money to do so. After paying the medical bills and the funeral costs, I bought a car and then stuffed the rest of the funds into an account with a financial advisor. I could have bought a house and lived carefree for a while, but that's not how I was raised. Instead, I have just enough released to me each month to cover rent and some basic needs while I work to keep busy.

That's why I'm working at the small time grocery store instead of pushing for something better. I finally get done with my third twelve-hour shift in as many days and instead of being able to relax, I have to find out what's going on with Russ's car. Granted, I'm the dumbass who didn't hand over the card to my neighbor on Friday morning when he came over asking about who he needs to call. I lied and told him that I misplaced it. On Saturday, I pretended that I had already called and they said it wasn't ready. Sunday gave me a convenient excuse to say they were closed.

In all fairness, a lot of small businesses in the area still like to be closed on Sundays. I remember my aunt used to tell me stories about when she was a kid and even the grocery stores would be closed on Sundays in Pennsylvania and that you couldn't buy alcohol at all on Sundays. I thought she was full of shit until I moved out here to Wrenshaw. Even as a suburb of Pittsburgh, there are a lot of businesses that still hold to the older ways with limited hours or being closed on Sundays.

After getting out of work at seven this morning, I ended up getting roped into taking Russel to his job downtown because I didn't sneak inside quickly enough. I felt guilty for withholding the information on his car, so it wasn't difficult for him to sucker me into the forty plus minute drive (without traffic) to get him to the First Avenue T Station. His office is right across the street from the Steel Building, but it's a bitch to drive in downtown Pittsburgh, especially having to navigate around the arena and the traffic coming off Veterans Bridge from the North Hills.

After dropping him off, it's past nine in the morning, so I figure I can take a chance and call the shop for Russ while I'm driving back home. It took over an hour to get here because of stupid rush hour. At least now that I'm going in the opposite direction of the people still fighting to get to work, it should be closer to the usual forty minutes.

"Good Boy T and T. This is Johnny."

I can't put my finger on why, but something in his voice as it surrounds me in the car is putting me on edge. Is this even the same guy? After I make sure I'm talking to the same man who I met the other night, I wrack my brain trying to figure out what's bothering me so much about this.

In between some sniffling, he outlines all of the things that would need fixing on Russel's car. It takes a minute for me to realize what's bothering me so much about his voice. It's not that he's sick. He's been crying.

My hands clench on the steering wheel while I'm stopped at the last light in Hazelwood before the bridge. I honestly can't say what has me more upset: the list of everything that is fucked up on my friend's car or that this man is struggling to hold back his emotions to do his job. By the time I'm across the river and heading through Homestead, Johnny has outlined everything.

"Basically, the car is worth more as scrap than as a vehicle right now," he manages with only a brief sniffle at the end. "It's not worth fixing unless there's senti-mental value and deep pockets."

I huff out a laugh at that. Does it have sentimental value? Yeah, kind of. Russ got that car as a huge "Fuck You" statement to his father when the old man didn't take kindly to his only son liking diapers and binkies as a grown man. It didn't help at the time that his new best friend and neighbor also happened to be a gay man. I think the only reason Dave didn't kick me out is the fact that Russ revealed his age play kink long before I moved in. Well, that and the fact that I don't fit the stereotype that Dave has in his head of what a gay man should look and act like.

"There's some sentimental value, but I don't think Russ will have a problem with scrapping it if that's what you say is the best thing to do," I tell him honestly. "He's not unreasonable and honestly I'd feel better about him driving if he wasn't in a pop can on wheels."

The sound coming through my speakers could only be him dropping the phone on his end, so I hold back my laughter while I wait to find out what it is that has the adorable mechanic so flustered. After some creative language is mumbled in the background, he lets out a long breath.

"I'll work on boxing everything from the interior for you then. Just send an email to the address on the card to let me know when you and your partner are ready to come by and get that and discuss how you want to handle the scrap process."

His voice is off again. It's almost robotic in its coldness. I want to correct his misconception that Russel and I are together, but a car cuts me off at the bridge and the call is disconnected by the time I'm done cussing out the rude jagoff that apparently learned to drive in some ass backward hick town. As soon as I'm away from the idiot, I try to ring the shop again. Obviously the number on the card is Johnny's direct line, and I need to clear this up as soon as fucking possible.

Voicemail.

At the next stoplight, I look up the main number for Good Boy Tinkering and Towing and anxiously drum my fingers on the wheel while it rings.

"Good Boy T and T. This is Paul."

Before I can say a word, there's a commotion on the other end.

"Hold on a second," he says and there's the sound of the phone being set down. In the background, there's the sound of voices and a slamming sound before this Paul gets back to me. "Sorry about that. How can I help you?"

Clearing my throat, I ask, "Is Johnny available? He's working on my neighbor's car."

"Sorry my man. He ain't in," Paul says happily. "The girlie colored car, right? Not sure how long Goose is gonna be here after fighting with the bossman, so you might want to pick someone else to work on your woman's ride."

Despite pulling into my driveway, I don't get out of the car. I'm trying to process exactly what the fuck this asshole is saying. There's some more background noise and the phone is obviously farther away when I hear his voice again.

"I never understood why the boss kept a guy like that around here anyways. Ain't no man that takes it up the ass gonna have what it takes to do this job."

I hang up the phone before I say something I'm going to really regret. Okay, so I won't regret saying it. I'll only regret the trip to the county jail after the resultant assault charges being brought against me for heading over there to beat the ever loving shit out of this homophobic jagoff who has the gall to speak ill of my boy.

He's not my...

Oh, fuck it. He is my boy even if he doesn't know it yet.